Run With the Hare

Linda Newbery

Run With the Hare

Lions

First published in Armada 1988
First published in Lions 1992

Lions is an imprint of the Children's Division,
part of HarperCollins Publishers Ltd,
77–85 Fulham Palace Road, Hammersmith,
London W6 8JB

Copyright © Linda Newbery 1988

The author asserts the moral right to be
identified as the author of this work

ISBN 0 00 692960-5

Printed and bound in Great Britain by
HarperCollins Manufacturing, Glasgow

Note to Readers

The system of veal production described in Chapter Four, where veal calves are reared in individual crates, became illegal in January 1990. This legislation has been brought about largely by the efforts of the various animal welfare organizations.

However, calves continue to be exported to similar rearing systems on the Continent, where there is no ban.

Foreword by Richard Adams

This promising first novel by a young writer gives an excellent idea of the feelings of ordinary young people who find themselves drawn to and involved in the Animal Rights movement. There is always the feeling that any personal effort is nothing but a drop in the ocean and that the individual can make little difference to the vast evil of present-day cruelty to animals. This, however, is not the case and I am in no doubt that by the 21st century a great change will have been brought about, largely through the united public efforts of people like Elaine and Kate, the very ordinary schoolgirl heroines of this novel.

Richard Adams

Chapter One

"What are we having for lunch today, then? Lentil sandwiches?"

Elaine glanced up at the speaker, Danny Webster, a member of the upper sixth, and then across the table at her friend Kate. It was impossible to predict Kate's reaction to this kind of remark. Having let it be widely known, on joining the sixth form at the start of term, that she was a strict vegetarian and Animal Rights campaigner, Kate was the constant target of jokes and taunts, some of them well-meaning, others less so. She had been known to respond by letting flow a savage torrent of rhetoric on the evils of factory farming or the dangers of food additives.

However, on this occasion Kate merely cast a scornful eye over the contents of Danny's tray, which he was unloading on to the table, and replied amiably, "Peanut butter, actually. Have one."

"Thanks, I prefer dead pig." To add emphasis to his words, Danny took a large mouthful of ham sandwich, making appreciative noises as he munched.

Elaine returned her attention to the careful unsealing of a yoghurt carton, aware as she did so that even a substance as innocuous as natural yoghurt would not escape Kate's wrath if she chose to give vent to it. Kate's vegetarianism took the extreme form of boycotting not only meat, but all products derived from animals: milk, cheese, yoghurt, eggs. Even her shoes were non-leather, and she refused to wear any garment made of wool. Elaine wondered idly what would have happened if her friend had joined the school earlier. The sixth form pupils were allowed to wear their own clothes, so Kate's habitual black garb adorned with Animal Rights badges, her scuffed black hockey boots and droopy black raincoat, while not actually approved of by the school's senior staff, were at least tolerated; as a junior pupil, though, she would have been expected to wear the regulation navy woollen blazer. It would have made an interesting confrontation, Elaine thought, recalling the headmaster's obsession with the finer points of uniform. She couldn't imagine Kate missing the chance of delivering a diatribe on the less pleasant aspects of sheep farming and its links with the slaughterhouse.

"Mind if I join you?" Another laden tray was dumped on the table, and the newcomer, Ann Wilcox, sat down without waiting for an answer and began eating rapidly.

"Got to hurry," she explained between mouthfuls. "I've got an English essay to finish before the bell goes. I suppose you two have done yours?" She glanced at Elaine and Kate, who were in the same A level set.

"If it's for Old Parsonage, you'd better make sure you get it done," Danny remarked. "He was in a foul mood this morning."

"He always is when he's had you upper sixth," Elaine commented. "What did you do to upset him this time?"

"It wasn't any of us," Danny retorted. "It was this new bloke who's joined the group. From the Adult Education Centre. Not that he's much older than us – only about twentyish, I should think."

"What did he do, then?" Kate had finished her peanut butter sandwiches and was unwrapping a muesli bar. "Old Parsonage can't complain at the adult students, can he, if they don't hand their work in on time? It's up to them."

"No, it wasn't that. It was in a discussion we were having. I don't want to bore you with the details," Danny remarked loftily. "I don't suppose you younger ones are sufficiently acquainted with the works of E. M. Forster to understand."

"Cut out the superior upper sixth intellectual stuff and just tell us what happened," Kate ordered.

"Well, this new bloke really seems to know his stuff, and he was putting Old Parsonage right on a few points, disagreeing with him in front of everyone *and* quoting from the book to back up what he said."

"But that's what Mr Parsonage always *wants* us to do," Elaine objected.

Danny grinned knowingly. "Yes, I know he *says* that, but you wait till you see him coming off worse in an argument."

"I can't begin to imagine it," said Elaine. "Who is this intellectual giant?"

"You've probably seen him around. Tall; short dark hair; dresses smartly. All the girls seem to think he's good-looking."

"Well, he sounds more interesting than the Adult Education people in our group," Elaine remarked. "We've got two women in their fifties called Dorothy and Rose who keep talking about what it was like when they were at school. Mr Parsonage keeps having to shut them up."

Mr Parsonage, in spite of the epithet which invariably accompanied his name, was in fact only in his late twenties. A recent recruit to Dodds Green Comprehensive, he oozed enthusiasm for literature but apparently had trouble in controlling the younger, more boisterous pupils. Elaine suspected that the A level lessons were the only ones in which he felt fully in control, and it must have been an unpleasant surprise to find himself confronted by a determined and knowledgeable opponent. The recent introduction of adult students into some of the A level classes was the result of a joint venture with the Adult Education Centre; the idea hadn't been greeted with much enthusiasm by the sixth form, but to Ann, who was leaning forward with both elbows on the table, her unfinished essay forgotten, the scheme clearly offered unexpected bonuses.

"This new guy – is he the one with the suede flying jacket?" she asked Danny.

"Yeah, that's the one. Mark someone."

"Oh, you mean Mark Harrington," Kate said. "I know him a bit, out of school."

"Really? Tell me more," Ann invited.

Before Kate could reply, an officious-looking dinner lady in a blue overall bore down on the group. "Come on, it's time we had all these tables cleared up," she told them irritably. "It's gone twenty-to."

"Oh, my *essay*," Ann wailed, as the others got to their feet and began collecting together trays and drink cartons. "I must dash. See you later."

Danny sauntered off in the direction of some fellow upper sixth, and Elaine and Kate made their way through the lunch tables, where several disgruntled second years were being made to pick up litter by a stony-faced dinner lady.

"How do you know this Mark character out of school?" Elaine asked Kate later that afternoon as they walked towards the bus stop at the end of the school road.

"Animal Rights," Kate replied, stepping aside to allow a noisy group of third years to pass. "He's a fairly new member. You'll probably see him on Thursday, if you come."

"Of course I'm coming. I said I would." Elaine remembered as she spoke that she hadn't mentioned the meeting to her parents yet. She wasn't sure how they would receive the idea. To most people, the term "Animal Rights" conjured up reports of the more extreme activities reported by the press: laboratory raids, break-ins at fur shops, letter bombs sent to research scientists.

"Come home with me after school on Thursday and we can make something to eat," Kate added. "That'll save you two bus journeys."

"Great. Thanks." Elaine thought briefly and with envy of the casual, friendly atmosphere of Kate's house, picturing the living room with its scattered cushions, newspapers, books, cats, and mugs of coffee. It was vastly different from her own home, where everything had to be polished and shiny and in its proper place. Elaine would never have issued a casual invitation to a friend to come for a meal, as Kate had just done, without checking with her parents first. But at the Ellisons', anyone could turn up unexpectedly at a meal time and an extra plate would be produced, without fuss or tutting.

"Here's your bus," said Kate. "See you tomorrow."

She was swept along the pavement in a navy-blue tide of Dodds Green pupils, her short stocky figure, surmounted by its untidy mop of fair hair, dwarfed by an overtaking group of lanky fifth year boys. Elaine boarded the bus amidst a gaggle of chattering children, sat down behind the driver and pulled out *Sons and Lovers* from her bag.

"Hi, Elaine," said a familiar voice. "I hoped I'd see you."

It was Alistair Marchant, a tall, slight boy with sandy hair which was always flopping into his eyes. He lived in Elaine's road, and they had for years shared an easy friendship. Like her, he was in the lower sixth, although they didn't cross paths much at school, as he was involved in computers and sciences whereas she was taking arts subjects. They occasionally went out together, on a fairly casual basis as far as Elaine was concerned.

Alistair sat down beside her as the bus pulled away and offered her a piece of chocolate. "How about coming round tonight? I've got a new video."

Elaine hesitated. "I've got an awful lot of homework. I think I ought to work tonight." Then, seeing the look of disappointment on Alistair's face, she felt mean. "Well . . . perhaps on second thoughts . . . if I do my work as soon as I get in –"

"Great!" Alistair's face brightened and he launched into an explanation of his choice of video film. Elaine listened at first, but found her thoughts wandering. She looked past Alistair and out of the opposite window, at the rows of terraced houses which gradually gave way to more spacious, tree-lined avenues, with horse chestnuts well into their autumn colours, as the bus drove into the outlying area of town where she and Alistair lived. She was conscious of a faint wish that Alistair hadn't got on the bus. It wasn't that she disliked him in any way – on the contrary – but she was becoming aware that he depended on the friendship far more than she did, and the thought made her feel unaccountably restless.

"See you later, then." They parted outside Alistair's gate, and Elaine walked on, the September sun warm on her back, the air heavy with the scent of late roses and mown grass. Warm enough to sit in the garden and do her homework, she decided, as she let herself into the empty house.

The air inside was cool after the warm sunshine. It was the cleaning lady's day, and everything was spotless, the faint furrow marks of the vacuum cleaner still visible in the jade-green hall carpet. In the kitchen, Elaine found a note from her mother: "Please set oven No. 4 and put casserole in. Onions etc. ready for yours in pan. Start cooking rice 6.15. In about 6.30. Mum."

Hating the silence, Elaine turned on the radio for company and, her homework forgotten, began to think about cooking. A look in the saucepan revealed some chopped onions and peppers, and she went to the rack to select further ingredients to make a vegetable casserole for herself. One penalty of her decision to follow Kate's lead and become vegetarian was that she now had to cook her own meals. Her mother, who worked full-time as a buyer in a London department store, was impatient with "food faddists", as she called them, and had her own domestic routines too firmly established for her to tolerate such an apparently eccentric deviation.

By the time Elaine's father came in, the supper was under control, and Elaine had almost finished her history notes. Mrs George arrived a few minutes later, immaculate in a well-cut cream suit. She kissed Elaine absently and asked whether she had had a good day, at the same time opening her mail. Elaine remembered that her parents were going out for drinks with friends, so they would be in a hurry. They had such a busy social life that it often seemed to her that she didn't see much of them, only meeting them in the mornings or as they passed through in the evenings on their way in or out.

Over the meal, Elaine mentioned Thursday's meeting, tactfully describing it as an "animal welfare" meeting rather than giving the impression of anything less respectable.

"What is it, the RSPCA?" Mr George asked. "Old ladies with pet poodles?"

"No, nothing as formal as that."

Mrs George's elegant features were drawn into a frown of suspicion. "It's not one of those groups that throw bombs through scientists' windows and inject turkeys with poison?" She had already indicated her reservations about Elaine's friendship with Kate, expressing disapproval of Kate's scruffy appearance and her possible influence on Elaine.

"Of course not. I don't want to get involved in anything like that."

"Is Alistair going?" Mrs George was far more ready to encourage Alistair as a companion for her daughter, seeing him as entirely steady and reliable.

"No. It's his rehearsal night. Anyway, I don't think he'd be interested."

"More sense, probably," said Mr George.

"Well, be careful." Elaine's mother got up from the

15

table and studied her make-up in the mirror on the kitchen wall. "I don't want you getting into any trouble."

"I told you, there won't *be* any trouble," Elaine assured her. However, she reflected that she actually knew very little about the other people who would be at the meeting, or what they were likely to be involved in. She told herself that Kate, ardent as she was, surely wouldn't want a part in anything illegal or likely to harm anyone.

Nevertheless, by the time Thursday evening came, she felt distinctly anxious.

She brushed her thick dark brown hair, which was unfashionably long despite her mother's urgings to try a more sophisticated style, in front of the mirror in Kate's cluttered bedroom. Frowning critically at her reflection, she wondered what sort of impression she would give a group of strangers.

"Come on, you look quite beautiful enough." Kate rarely paid much attention to her appearance beyond running her hands impatiently through her thick unruly mop of corkscrew curls. She was collecting together leaflets and press cuttings.

"Seen this one?" She offered Elaine a leaflet which pictured a wide-eyed black-and-white calf in a veal unit.

"No."

"It's the latest campaign. They'll be talking about it tonight."

Elaine took the leaflet and read it quickly. It had been just such a leaflet which had made her become vegetarian, only a few weeks ago. Until then she had considered herself an animal lover, but had never given much thought to the methods by which the meat arrived on the table in front of her each meal time. She had been horrified to discover the facts which were, it seemed, deliberately concealed from the general public. Knowing the truth only made her feel completely powerless to change anything, but, she reminded herself, that was why she was going to the meeting – to meet other people who felt the same.

She had forgotten about Mark Harrington, the subject of the lunch time conversation, but when they arrived at the meeting – in the front room of someone's house – he was the first person she saw. She recognized him at once, having passed him in the corridor at school a few times. The first thing that struck her now was how much smarter he looked than most of the other people present. His straight dark brown hair was neatly cut, rather short, and he wore a white shirt and navy-blue tie under his grey suede jacket. The thought struck Elaine that the latter was rather an odd choice of garment for an Animal Rights meeting. She had spent some time worrying over her own leather shoes, and was hoping that no one would notice them and denounce her as a hypocrite.

Kate was making introductions. "This is Elaine, a new member. This is Joe, who organizes things; Maureen; Stuart; Sue; Mark you've probably seen . . .'

Elaine smiled briefly at each person Kate indicated. She was surprised by the age range, having expected everyone to be her age or slightly older. Joe, who was thin and bearded and wore a sweat shirt with the wording, "Fur coats are worn by beautiful animals and ugly people", looked about thirty, and there were two women, Maureen and Sue, who were probably older than that, as well as a grey-haired couple, Mr and Mrs Wiseman, who must have been in their sixties. Joe, who sat at a dining table with wallet folders and papers spread in front of him, smiled at Elaine and said, "Pleased you could come. We're always glad of new members."

Maureen, who wore a pale blue boiler suit and a CND earring, smiled too, and fetched Elaine a seat so that she could sit next to Kate. On the other side of Kate sat the boy introduced as Stuart, who looked pleasant, with straight fair hair and a friendly, open expression. He was,

17

Elaine knew, a very close friend of Kate's, though she had never met him before.

By the time several more people had arrived and seats or floor cushions been found for them, the room seemed very crowded. Kate was deep in conversation with Stuart, so Elaine studied a factory farming leaflet which had been handed to her. She looked up to find Mark Harrington's eyes on her from the opposite side of the room. She responded with an uncertain smile, but he immediately looked away and said something to the person next to him.

"OK, let's get started." Joe's raised voice cut across the general chatter, and gradually everyone fell silent.

"There's quite a few things coming up, but first the new factory farming campaign," Joe began. "You'll all have seen the new leaflets by now –" he held them up "– and there are various posters. The campaign starts on Saturday with leafletting in the precinct and writing to MPs. Then, as it gets nearer to Christmas, we'll concentrate on the turkey leaflets and some of us will be joining in the usual march to the Royal Smithfield Show."

"I'm no good at writing letters," said someone.

"There'll be sample letters passed round later. You can base yours on those, if you're not sure," Joe explained. "Now, let's sort out Saturday. The idea is to hand out leaflets on chicken batteries and veal units in the precinct from ten o'clock onwards. We'll carry on all day in shifts if we can get enough people. I'll bring the posters and placards along and we'll try to get people to sign a petition. How many of you think you can make it?"

Several hands were raised and Maureen began to make a list of names and times.

"Do you want to do some?" Kate asked Elaine. "How about the afternoon? I've got my Saturday job in the morning."

"Yes, fine." Elaine felt sure that handing out leaflets in

the precinct couldn't possibly be categorized by her mother as getting into trouble.

"Put Elaine and me down for the afternoon," Kate told Maureen.

"That looks like quite a good turnout," said Joe, looking pleased.

"That's all very well, but can't we do something a bit more direct?" asked someone. "We're always handing out leaflets, but it doesn't get anything changed."

There were a few murmurs of agreement, and Elaine turned to look at the speaker, a powerful, thick-set youth in his early twenties, with a belligerent expression and short, stubbly fair hair.

"What have you got in mind?" Jo asked, rather warily, Elaine thought.

The fair boy shrugged. "A raid or something. Or how about a sit-in at the slaughterhouse?"

"Where *is* the nearest slaugherhouse?" someone asked.

"There's one over at Five Elms," replied a girl with thick jet-black hair. "Terry and all them tried before. They're a right rough lot though, the slaughtermen, I mean."

"Yeah, and how. But if enough of us go we'll get in. They won't be able to stop us," said the fair youth.

"Or if we go at night we could try to get some animals out," added the girl. "You could get Jason and all them blokes from over Northwood, couldn't you, Tel?"

Elaine was beginning to feel rather disturbed by the turn the conversation was taking, but, to her relief, Maureen steered the conversation back into safer waters by saying, "Well, I think we should finish Joe's arrangements first. I'm not breaking into the slaughterhouse at night, and I can't see much point in getting arrested for having a sit-in there, where no one can even see us. I'll stick to the leafletting and letter-writing."

The black-haired girl gave a disgusted snort. Joe tried to

smooth things over. "Look, we agreed – or at least most of us did – that the purpose of this group is to bring various issues to the public's attention by peaceful means – leafletting and demonstrations and so on. There are various groups who get involved in more – let's say – direct action. If Terry and Sandra want to organize something, then there's no reason why they shouldn't. But I think they should organize that on their own, separately from the group. Now, about the letter-writing . . ."

As the meeting progressed, Elaine formed the impression that there were two distinct factions in the group. When the start of the forthcoming hunting season was mentioned, Joe's suggestion of a banner demonstration at the opening meet was greeted with scorn by Terry and his followers.

"What's the good of that? Whose mind are you going to change?"

"The idea is," Joe explained patiently, "to get some publicity in the local press, so that it's brought to the attention of the public."

"I suppose you'd rather bring in all your Northwood acquaintances and have a repeat of last year's little incident," Maureen said acidly.

Terry glowered at her. "At least we *do* something."

Maureen was furious. "I like that! How many letters have you written during the last month?"

Joe was looking anxiously from one to the other. "Now let's not argue among ourselves. That'll get us nowhere. Presumably, Terry, you'd like to do some sabbing? Well, I'm not averse to a little sabbing myself – providing it's *organized*. I'd rather avoid a repeat of last year. But there's no reason why we can't combine that with a demonstration at the meet. Some people might prefer to come just for that. Who'd be interested in the demonstration?"

A few hands went up, and Joe looked relieved. Elaine,

who had never seen foxhounds before, raised her hand, feeling that it would be a good opportunity to see what went on without committing herself to anything too drastic. She wondered what exactly had happened the year before.

Joe went on to talk briefly about a few items of interest in the local and national press, after which Maureen and Stuart took orders for tea and coffee, and the meeting dissolved into general chatting.

As she accepted a mug from the tray, Elaine overheard Stuart on her right telling Kate, "Mark says it's OK for Sunday." Puzzled – Kate hadn't mentioned anything happening on Sunday – Elaine sipped her coffee. Her gaze fell on Mark, who seemed to be doodling on a notepad. He hadn't said a single word during the entire meeting. Strange, Elaine thought, for someone with the reputation of being an extrovert intellectual.

Chapter Two

"I'm just going down to the town," Elaine called from the hall.

"Oh, Elaine, I wish you'd told me you were going. I had to go in this morning especially to collect something from the dry cleaners. I could have asked you to get it for me," said Mrs George, appearing from the kitchen with a cookery book in her hand.

"Sorry, didn't think to mention it. I'm meeting Kate," Elaine explained.

"Oh. Well, don't be back late, will you? The Hammonds are coming for supper, so you'll need to change into something reasonable." She looked critically at Elaine's blue jeans and green striped rugby shirt.

Elaine's heart sank at the mention of the Hammonds. They were among the most irritating of her parents' friends, Mrs with her brittle, nerve-jolting laugh, and Mr reeking of cigars and overpowering aftershave. Perhaps she could escape to her room as soon as the meal was over, on the pretext of having an essay to write. She walked towards the bus stop, past the carefully-tended front gardens with their Japanese maples and staked clumps of chrysanthemums. It was another warm afternoon, with little to suggest that autumn was approaching.

She met Kate at the bookshop and they made their way through the Saturday shopping crowd towards the main precinct, where large chain stores jostled for attention with small jewellers and bakers and newsagents. A few people were handing out leaflets rather despondently. Joe's posters, mounted on hardboard, were propped against the edge of a raised stone flowerbed. A few shoppers stopped to gaze at them curiously.

"Thought no one else was ever coming," Stuart complained. "We've been here ages." He handed his stack of leaflets to Kate.

"Are you all clearing off and leaving us to it?" said Kate in resigned tones, dumping her patchwork fabric shoulder bag on the edge of the flowerbed.

"Yes, I've got to go and collect the van from the garage, and I'm giving Adrian and Jane a lift. Maureen and Sue are supposed to be coming along later. Here's the petition. I don't know if Mark's going to leave off yet – he's only been here about half an hour." Following the direction of his glance, Elaine saw Mark Harrington, with his back to them, offering a leaflet to a woman with a pushchair. "Mark!" Stuart called. "You're not going yet, are you?"

Mark turned round. "No, I can stay a bit longer. Hi, Kate. Hello," he said to Elaine, glancing at her briefly.

Elaine felt vaguely disconcerted by his presence. She didn't know why. She remembered Danny saying at school that all the girls thought him good-looking. He was, rather, she thought, and his height – he must be six feet – gave him an air of distinction, but it wasn't his looks so much as a somehow enigmatic, reserved quality that made him seem different from other boys she knew.

She picked up a pile of leaflets, which pictured chickens in batteries, and Kate said, "If anyone seems interested, ask if they'd like to sign the petition. I'll leave it here."

Elaine took up a stand just outside the newsagents, where there seemed to be a fairly constant stream of people going in and out, and held out her first leaflet, rather tentatively, towards the first person who approached. The young smartly-dressed woman simply glanced at the leaflet and veered away, as if she thought she was being asked for money. Elaine wondered whether she was

23

supposed to address the passers-by, explain what she was doing. She looked across at Mark, who was standing outside the menswear shop facing approaching shoppers with a diffident half-smile. He was smartly dressed, as before, in his suede jacket and blue tie, making Elaine feel scruffy by comparison. He suddenly turned and caught her eye as she gazed at him and she looked away quickly, not wanting him to think she was like some of the girls at school, who were absorbedly interested in boys to the exclusion of all other subjects. She thrust out a leaflet at a passing shopper who took it, rather startled.

Two teenage girls actually approached her in order to take copies, and Elaine felt heartened. She experimented with various techniques as the shopping crowd grew more dense towards the busy mid-afternoon peak. Eye-contact was the main thing, she discovered, although some people still swerved away defensively. But one or two looked at the leaflets and said, "Well done, keep up the good work," or made other encouraging comments.

Watching the endless procession of shoppers flowing towards her and diverging like the current of a stream round a boulder, Elaine was struck by the enormity of the task before her. What hope was there of animating people *en masse* into giving any consideration to the way their meat appeared neatly sliced and packaged on the supermarket shelves, let alone provoking them into wanting to do anything about it? Most of the faces passing her looked either expressionless or intent on the next purchase. Yet each person was an individual with interests and worries and family ties. The thought intrigued her. It seemed to put her own sense of self-importance into perspective, like looking at the stars in a clear night sky and feeling suddenly diminished to the size of a pinhead.

Slow as progress seemed, she eventually reached her last leaflet and went back to the box for more. Kate was talking to someone who was signing the petition, two teenage boys were looking at the placards, and Mark was sitting on the stone edge of the flowerbed, apparently writing in a notebook. He always seemed to be writing things down – like Hamlet, Elaine remembered from her A level lessons, setting things down in his tablets. Perhaps Mark was writing a novel. That would explain his air of preoccupation and remoteness.

The box of leaflets was three-quarters empty; Elaine took the remaining ones and resumed her position. A grey-haired woman, peering short-sightedly, said, "Oh, no. I can't look at anything like that. I love animals," and marched decisively away, probably on her way to buy pork chops for supper, Elaine thought savagely. Why didn't people want to know? But she knew the answer. It was easier to go on thinking you were an animal lover, without considering the contradictions involved: you couldn't call yourself an animal lover while eating the creatures you claimed to love. She checked herself, remembering that she had been exactly the same until a few weeks ago.

The leaflets ran out before the next shift arrived. "Maureen will have lots more. We'll have to wait till she comes to give her the petition and the placards," Kate said.

Mark, who had stopped writing, stood up, leaving his notebook on the low wall next to Kate's bag, and said he was going to buy a newspaper.

Kate flopped down by the geraniums. "I hate standing in one place," she remarked. "Give me a cross-country run any day." She picked up Mark's notebook and flipped through the pages.

Elaine was outraged. "You can't do that! It might be private!"

Kate wasn't listening, intently studying one of the pages. "Crikey, look at this! It's you!"

Startled, Elaine sneaked a glance, overwhelmed with

curiosity yet afraid that Mark would come back and see them prying into his book. It was a sketch book, not writing as she had imagined. She saw at once that Kate was right. It was a full-page drawing of herself, instantly recognizable with her jeans and sweatshirt and long hair, and even holding the leaflets, but given, with the deft pencil strokes, the remote, abstracted air of a Pre-Raphaelite beauty.

"Shut it, quick!" she hissed.

But Kate continued to hold the book open, looking up at Elaine in amusement. "It's jolly flattering," she remarked. "He —"

Elaine snatched the book from her and placed it, firmly shut, back on the wall.

"Hello, you two," said a female voice beside them. "Having a break?"

Elaine turned guiltily as Kate greeted Maureen and Sue. "The relief shift. About time. We've run out of leaflets, and we've almost filled up the petition."

"Well, we'll take over until the shops close," said Maureen, nodding at Mark as he reappeared with the *Guardian*.

"Great," said Kate. "Time for a cup of tea in Parker's. Coming, Mark?"

"OK," Mark said diffidently. Elaine didn't dare look at him.

Parker's was the local department store, very staid, with the tearoom usually full of ladies in hats. Elaine wondered at Kate's choice, but all became clear when Kate led the way through Haberdashery and into Ladies' Fashions to search for real fur coats. "Just in case we need to have a demonstration. They'll be getting their winter stock in," she explained.

All the fur coats proved to be fakes; whether this pleased Kate, or whether she was disappointed because there would now be no need for a demonstration, it was difficult to tell.

"Come on," Mark urged. "That assistant is giving us a

funny look. You do look a bit incongruous in here among the Crimplene two-piece suits."

They found an empty table in the corner of the tearoom, weaving their way through the shopping bags and snatches of conversations. Kate studied the menu, her elbows on the starched white tablecloth. "Black tea for me. They've never heard of vegans in here."

The waitress came, in a white frilly apron and matching cap, and Mark did the ordering as if it were naturally taken for granted that he should. Elaine knew that this would annoy Kate who disliked such assumptions, considering herself a feminist. But she rather liked Mark's air of assurance. If she'd been out with Alistair, they'd have done the ordering between them, with much hesitation and double-checking, while the waitress hovered impatiently.

"Still got your job?" Kate asked Mark when the waitress had gone.

"Yes. It's completely deadly, but it brings in some money. I wish I could find something less stultifying." He had a pleasant voice, Elaine thought, low-pitched and intelligent.

"What do you do?" Elaine asked, looking at him directly for the first time since her embarrassment over the drawing.

"I work in a bank, apart from the two mornings when I'm in school." Their eyes met across the table. His were an unusual colour, she noticed, a sort of dark green-brown with lighter flecks. She looked away with a conscious effort. She wondered why he did something as boring as working in a bank, and why he only had a part-time job, but felt it might be rather too blunt to ask.

"Mark's an artist," Kate said as though answering the unspoken question.

"Really?" Elaine was impressed. She had never met a real artist apart from Mr Rose, the art teacher at school, who was generally considered to be a bit dotty.

Mark laughed self-deprecatingly. "What Kate means is that I managed to sell a few paintings at the summer Art

27

Exhibition. They haven't asked me to put on a one-man show at the Hayward yet."

"Elaine paints, as well," Kate volunteered, in her self-appointed role as conversational go-between.

Elaine glared at her. "I'm doing A level art at school," she explained to Mark, in case he should think she sold paintings too.

The tea arrived on a silver tray and Kate assembled the cups and saucers. "Milk?" she asked the other two pointedly. Mark accepted, which meant he wasn't vegan like Kate, Elaine noted, although presumably a vegetarian.

Kate poured out the two cups of tea with milk and a black one for herself. "How are you enjoying the English lessons?" she asked Mark.

"Oh, it's OK, I suppose. The set books are quite interesting. I'm surprised we're not expected to do more background reading though. And the discussions aren't noted for their stimulating qualities. Some of the students never say anything at all."

"It's probably having older, knowledgeable men-of-the-world like yourself present," Kate remarked. "It inhibits them."

Mark laughed again, scornfully, showing very white, slightly uneven teeth. Elaine found herself studying him again, taking in the details of his appearance. His skin looked smooth, lightly-tanned against the crisp whiteness of his shirt. He looked as if he dressed carefully, making sure everything matched. His clothes weren't fashionable, but they looked expensive. She wondered how he could afford to be fussy about clothes, only working part-time. Perhaps he sold his paintings for fabulous prices. She imagined him working in a cellar in a paint-stained smock, frowning intently at a huge canvas covered in abstract blotches.

Kate refilled Mark's and Elaine's teacups and then

looked at her watch. "Crikey, is that the time? I must get to the library before it closes. I'll see you on Monday, Elaine." She was pushing her chair back and gathering up her bag before Elaine could protest.

"See you tomorrow," said Mark, and Kate set off through the crowded tables.

Elaine could have strangled her. She felt sure Kate had deliberately engineered the situation, leaving her sitting alone with Mark. It must be her idea of a joke, because she knew Elaine was embarrassed about the drawing. Elaine felt tongue-tied and awkward, searching her mind for something flippant to say to cover her confusion. But Mark didn't appear to be in the least perturbed; he sat back in his chair, relaxed, as if he had the entire evening to spare.

"What sort of things do you paint?" he asked Elaine, looking at her with a directness which she found disconcerting but somehow flattering.

"Oh . . . landscapes . . . people . . . nothing very good," she faltered. "What about you?"

"All sorts of things, really. Oils, acrylics, ink sometimes – fairly expressionist sort of stuff. I'm interested in photography, too, black-and-white."

Elaine didn't know much about photography, and couldn't think of anything to say about it. "How did you get involved in Animal Rights?" she asked instead.

"Through a friend at college. I designed some posters for a play they were doing at college and then this friend asked me to do some publicity work for the Animal Rights group. I started going along to the meetings and since then I've taken some photographs for them as well."

It all sounded very impressive to Elaine, designing posters and having work commissioned and selling paintings, a far cry from the splodgy watercolours she turned out under Mr Rose's supervision. But she couldn't quite see how it fitted in with doing English A level at school with a lot of adolescent sixth formers. "Why are you . . . I mean, what's the point of doing the English at school?" she asked hesitantly.

"It's the Adult Education Scheme. I've done evening classes with them before, life drawing and so on, and this year I thought I'd do English A level, to discipline myself a bit. I can't spend all my free time painting." He leaned forward, clasping his hands in front of him on the tablecloth. They were not at a¹ what Elaine would have thought of as artist's hands, but large, with broad, flat, scrupulously clean fingernails. "They don't have A level evening classes, so if you want to do one you have to go into school. I might go on and do an Open University degree afterwards, or even go to university full-time. A lot of them encourage you to do something else for a bit rather than go straight from school, so I won't be too old. What about you? What are you going to do when you've done your A levels?"

"I don't know." It was the question that was always being asked by teachers, parents and relatives, who seemed to expect you to have your entire career mapped out by the time you were fourteen. So far, Elaine had resisted her mother's urgings to take a business course, but had nothing positive to offer instead, beyond a vague feeling that she might like something to do with animals. ("But you should be taking biology and zoology and suchlike, if that's what you want to do, not arts subjects," Kate had pointed out when they had discussed it.) "It all seems so far away still. I've only just started the lower sixth," she replied to Mark's question. She was very conscious of his gaze on her. She felt flattered by his attentiveness towards someone who must seem a mere schoolgirl to someone of his age and experience. Perhaps he had been brought up to behave with perfect manners at all times, no matter how bored he may feel. She was becoming charmed by him, she realized, in spite of her

30

initial wariness, and she told herself abruptly not to be so silly. He had plenty of admiring girls to choose from. She thought of Polonius telling Ophelia in *Hamlet*, "He is a prince, out of thy star."

He paid for the tea and they emerged into the late afternoon sunshine, where the last shoppers were drifting away, leaving the precinct littered with sweet wrappers and pages from newspapers.

"Well, goodbye," Elaine said at the shop doorway, where sales assistants were standing pointedly, ready to lock up.

Mark hesitated, then said diffidently, "I was just wondering . . . there's a new exhibition of paintings opening at the Arts Centre on Friday. There's a preview in the evening, with food and wine. Some of my friends will be exhibiting. I don't suppose you'd like to go? I've got some tickets."

Elaine stopped dead, thinking that her ears must be deceiving her, or that she must be dreaming. But Mark was standing there, tall and solid and very real, waiting for an answer. She felt that her expression must betray her astonishment and – she realized – her delight at such an invitation. But she heard her voice answering, very calm and controlled, "Thank you – I'd love to come."

She caught the bus home, feeling capable even of facing an evening with the Hammonds.

Chapter Three

Coming across Kate in the sixth form common room at morning break on Monday, Elaine remembered that she had been involved in something mysterious the day before.

"Do anything interesting yesterday?" she asked casually.

Kate grinned mischievously. "You'll hear all about it soon enough," was all she would say.

Elaine was left to ponder. She wondered for a moment whether Kate might have been involved in a laboratory break-in, a dramatic raid to save animals earmarked for gruesome experiments. But surely if she had been about to embark on something as serious as that, she wouldn't have been so calm on Saturday. And Mark had obviously been involved as well. Elaine couldn't quite picture him cleaving his way through wire fencing, anonymous and menacing in a black balaclava. She felt a little hurt that Kate hadn't let her in on the secret. Perhaps she had yet to prove herself as a serious Animal Rights campaigner.

Remembering Joe's insistence on the importance of writing to MPs, she embarked on a letter-writing project. It seemed a serious undertaking, writing to a remote figure associated dimly in her mind with Parliamentary debates on the economy and foreign affairs. Incredible to think that someone involved in matters of such importance would actually read her letter, and not only read it but write a reply – Joe had seemed certain that MPs were bound to reply to letters from their constituents. She would write to the Prime Minister too, she decided, amused at the sudden mental picture of the letter being delivered by special messenger in the middle of a Commons debate, the Prime Minister silencing all the MPs with their braying voices familiar from Radio 4, and announcing, "I suggest, honourable friends, that we give this matter our urgent attention."

In reality, the process seemed horribly slow, from the information Elaine had gleaned from a pamphlet picked up at the meeting. If enough letters were received, then the local MP would bring up the matter in the House of Commons. But even then nothing was guaranteed. Elaine knew that much from a book on blood sports she'd borrowed from Kate. Apparently several Bills to ban hare coursing had been discussed in the House of Commons, only to be rejected by the House of Lords – "old fogeys with a couple of hunters each back in the shires, most likely," as Kate dismissively termed them. "They won't do anything likely to end up with a ban on fox-hunting."

Elaine thought of these lumbering, grinding wheels of legislative change as she began drafting her letter on factory farming. Millions of animals would live out their dreary days in battery houses and intensive rearing systems before a single law would be changed to improve their conditions. She could understand why some campaigners preferred to take more decisive action rescuing animals, not sitting indoors writing letters.

She had found out the name of her local MP from the town hall, and recognized it from local newspaper articles about the opening of the Arts Centre and visits to the new spinal injuries unit at the hospital. Elaine wondered how interested he was likely to be in chickens. It was difficult to know exactly what sort of tone to use for her letter, and she started and restarted several times, wishing she had remembered to look at Joe's samples at the meeting. Eventually she rejected emotive descriptions in favour of facts gathered from the various leaflets. She ended, "I do hope you will think this subject is important enough to raise in the House of Commons," and enclosed a leaflet for good measure. She copied out the same letter, with a few minor variations, and addressed it to 10 Downing Street.

"What on earth are you writing to the Prime Minister for?" Alistair asked, glimpsing the letter as she took it out of her bag and thrust it into the pillar box on the way to the bus stop next morning.

"It's about factory farming. The new campaign," she told him.

Alistair looked amused. "You must be mad. You'll never change anything. Most people don't give a damn about factory farming as long as it means they get their pork sausages and chicken joints."

"That doesn't mean you have to sit back and do nothing. How do you think women got the vote?" she flared back. "And at least you can stop buying the sausages and the chickens."

"Yes, but we don't all like lentil burgers."

"Oh – " Elaine thrust both hands into her jacket pockets, biting back a retort. There was no point in arguing with Alistair. He regarded her new interest in Animal Rights as a mild and probably transient eccentricity. When she had tried to explain her reasons for being a vegetarian, he had replied, "Yes, but the animals are already dead, so it makes no difference whether you buy the meat or not," and, "At least they've had a life." Elaine had heard much the same line of reasoning from her own parents. It was so smug and illogical, and showed such a lack of imagination, that she could only despair.

Alistair asked her how the evening with the Hammonds had been, and, recognizing that he was trying to compensate for needling her, she enquired about the rehearsals for the Youth Orchestra Concert.

"Fine. You will come to the concert, won't you? I'll get you a ticket." Alistair dug in his pocket for his fare as the bus drew up, crowded with schoolchildren and shoppers.

"Yes, thank you."

34

They climbed up to the upper deck, on a level with the yellowing horse chestnut leaves which brushed the windows with gentle fingers as the bus moved away.

"How about going to see the new film at the ABC on Friday?" Alistair asked.

Elaine thought of Friday with a sudden rush of secret excitement. "Oh, thanks, but I can't. I'm going to an art exhibition."

"Oh." Alistair looked despondent. "With the school?"

"No, with one of the Animal Rights members actually." She changed the subject back to the orchestral concert, not wanting to explain further. She knew that Alistair wouldn't like the idea of her going out with someone else, but then, she told herself defiantly, he had no claims on her. They were only friends.

On Friday evening she hurried home from school to wash and dry her hair, and then looked through her wardrobe critically, wondering which garments would be suitable to wear to an art exhibition. She thought it would be more appropriate to look romantic and Bohemian rather than trendy, and tried on three different outfits before finally choosing a calf-length mauvish printed skirt, a deep blue jumper in fine wool, and a white blouse with a high neck. She frowned at her reflection in the mirror, considering that she looked too ordinary for someone of Mark's sophistication, and added a finely-wrought silver brooch at her neck and a lacy blue-grey scarf, which echoed the colour of her eyes. That was better, she decided, giving her hair a final brushing.

"Where are you going, dressed like a Gypsy?" her mother, arriving home from work, asked suspiciously.

"Only to the exhibition at the Arts Centre." Elaine pulled on her grey jacket and felt in the pocket for her purse.

"Have you had anything to eat?"

35

"Oh, yes thanks." In fact Elaine had felt too nervous to eat much at all, and her stomach was by now churning with a mixture of hunger and anxiety. It was ridiculous to get so worked up, she told herself sternly. To Mark it was probably just an ordinary evening.

She waited in the front room, where she could see the road outside. Mark had said he would pick her up in his car, and she wanted to intercept him before he rang at the door, so that she wouldn't have to introduce him to her mother. It would be a new experience for her, going out with someone who had his own car. Before, it had always been buses or lifts from parents.

The hands of the clock crawled round. Elaine picked up the local paper and tried to read it, but her concentration was non-existent. Perhaps he wasn't going to come. Perhaps he'd forgotten about asking her, or had decided to go with someone else. But before many minutes had passed, the sound of a car approaching very fast made her look up to see a white Mini pulling up outside with a squeal of brakes.

"Bye." Elaine was out of the front door before her mother had time to comment. As she hurried down the path, she wondered whether perhaps she should have waited indoors, after all, to avoid looking too childish and eager.

Mark was standing by the open driver's door, smiling and relaxed. "Hi. I'm not late, am I?"

"Oh, no." She got into the car, trying to appear calm and casual and sophisticated.

Mark drove fast, with great flair, resting one hand on his knee. He was dressed with his usual elegance, in a pair of neatly-creased dark grey trousers with a lighter grey jacket, a pristine white shirt and a purplish tie. The car radio was on, not Radio 1, which would have been the choice of most of Elaine's contemporaries, but something Radio 3-ish with a harp and flute, very soothing.

"How was your week at school?" he asked her.

It was an ordinary enough remark, but accompanied by a sidelong glance from the green-brown eyes, very intense in the gloom of the car interior. Elaine felt disarmed, very conscious of his physical closeness.

"Oh, average. Lots of essays to write. All the teachers are really piling on the homework." She wished she could think of something wittier and more entertaining to say.

"What subjects are you taking, besides art?"

"History and English."

They discussed the set books for English. The upper sixth were studying different ones, but Mark seemed to have read most of the books the lower sixth had been set, which added to Elaine's sense of inadequacy. He seemed to have such a wide cultural background, able to talk easily about art and literature.

The Arts Centre stood on the edge of the town, overlooking the park. It was a modern building, raised on pillars, with a flight of steps leading to the plate glass entrance. The light from its large windows reflected on the lake, shimmering in the dusk. Elaine could see the silhouettes of people inside.

They mounted the steps, and Mark politely held open the glass door for her. Inside, through another set of doors, she could see long tables set with wine and food, paintings mounted on large screens, and many people already circulating. The lighting was subdued, with ceiling lights directed at the paintings, giving a glamorous aura to the room.

A middle-aged woman with long greyish hair swept up stylishly was waiting inside the inner door to greet guests as they arrived. Her glance swept past Elaine to Mark behind her, her face lighting with recognition. "Mark, how lovely to see you! You're not exhibiting this time, I see?"

"No, too busy with other things. This is Elaine." He placed a hand reassuringly on her shoulder. "This is Laura,

37

one of the pinions of the Art Society. You'll see some of her paintings in the exhibition."

"I've sold one already. Isn't it marvellous? Be sure not to miss Celia's sculptures, they're simply wonderful. Now do have some wine, and circulate," Laura urged gushingly, steering them towards one of the loaded tables.

"What will you have? White or red?" Mark turned to face Elaine, his dark hair burnished to a coppery sheen by the overhead lighting.

"White, please." She didn't usually like wine very much, but she took the glass Mark handed her and sipped it cautiously, surprised to find it sweet and flowery and refreshing.

They made their way towards the first of the screens, where several people were gathered, looking at the jewel-bright colours of some Mediterranean-looking landscapes in oils. The gallery was crowded now, and Elaine looked round at the other people, who ranged from elderly retired-colonel types in moustaches and tweeds to artistic-looking women in Indian silks and ethnic embroidery and expensive hand-knits. Elaine was impressed by the women, used to the flashy trendiness of her sixth form acquaintances in their bright high-street fashions; this seemed to her altogether more stylish.

She looked at the paintings thoughtfully. The conversations around her sounded like extracts from reviews in the arts section of the Sunday paper – "so atmospheric"; "Cezanne-like in the use of flat planes"; "terribly derivative, don't you think?" She felt inhibited from saying anything at all, unable to put her thoughts into the accepted jargon or to label things correctly. Fortunately, Mark didn't seem to expect her to say anything. He only glanced at the paintings rather dismissively, said "This sort of thing leaves me cold," and passed on to the next screen.

Elaine followed him towards a display of smaller watercolours. She felt immediately much more at home, having seen and admired several exhibitions of paintings like these in the local library. She studied them carefully, recognizing several local villages and viewpoints, and admiring the delicacy of tint and the capturing of light effects. She wished she could paint with such skill, envying the artist's ability of establishing with a few casual brush strokes a row of poplars seen through an early morning mist, or sunlight breaking through storm clouds, or purplish shadows falling across the rich warmth of a red-brick wall. She had forgotten Mark, until his voice cut into her thoughts. "The inevitable washy watercolours. People keep churning them out, year after year, exactly the same."

She straightened up, stung, as hurt as if the paintings had been her own by his dismissal of the beautiful subtlety of colouring and the atmospheric rendering of light and shade as mere "washy watercolours". She decided against admitting that she thought them beautiful, afraid that he would consider her boring and ignorant.

"What sort of things do you like, then?" she asked instead.

"I like a more individual approach, more expressive, paintings that say something. These are just technique, straight out of *Teach Yourself Watercolour Painting*. You can't tell one person's work from another." He waved a derisive hand towards the pictures, and it occurred to Elaine that he ought to be more careful; after all, the painter might be standing behind them listening for all he knew. "And it's such a dated style – there's nothing new and exciting about it. These pictures could have been done by Cotman and the Norfolk School."

Elaine frowned, thoroughly out of her depth and unable to argue. She had vaguely heard the name, Cotman but nothing further came to mind; from the sarcastic way in which Mark mentioned the name, she gathered that he was someone to be despised.

"Now this is much more interesting," Mark continued,

leading her on to confront some larger canvases portraying stocky, solid figures that looked like building labourers, executed in warm tones of brick-red crayon. "Look at the solidity, the three-dimensional quality of the figures. Don't you find that expressive?"

Elaine looked, not altogether sure what he meant by the term "expressive" – expressive of what? – except that it conjured up the name of Munch. She made a mental note to look it up in the *Dictionary of Art* at school. She had to admit that the drawing did have something compelling about it, a sort of weightiness and volume about the figures, a sense of the roundness of the limbs and the rough texture of the clothing. "Yes, I can see why you like it," she agreed. But she still didn't understand why she couldn't like the watercolours as well.

They moved on, Mark looking closely at another reddish crayon drawing, evidently by the same artist. Elaine felt discomfited by Mark's superior knowledge and the realization that she was neither confident nor articulate enough to convince him of the reasons for her own preferences. She looked back towards the spurned landscapes and her glance was distracted by a dramatically attractive girl, who was standing thoughtfully sipping wine. She was small and slender, with short, slightly spiky black hair, and was simply dressed in a baggy scarlet sweater and a tight black skirt. She looked up, caught Elaine's glance, and then focused on Mark, her dark eyes showing recognition and pleasure.

"Mark! I haven't seen you for ages!" She hurried over, reached her free arm around his neck and kissed him, standing on tiptoe.

Mark looked just as pleased, clasping her for a moment and looking down into her face. "Zoë! How are you?"

"Fine, thanks. The classes haven't been at all the same since you stopped coming, you know." She spoke in a teasing tone which made Elaine wonder if they knew each other very well.

"Yes, well, I have to spread my favours around, to keep everyone happy. I've been a bit busy lately." Mark's eyes were fixed on the girl's face in a way which made Elaine feel excluded.

"Yes, so I hear. Suzanna told me you'd got involved in Animal Rights. Is it true? I keep expecting to hear you've been arrested."

Elaine looked at the girl while she was speaking, noticing that her large brown eyes were fringed by long feathery lashes, and that her skin was pale and flawless. She felt large and clumsy and oafish by comparison.

"Yes. I'm doing something this Sunday as it happens, taking photographs. This is Elaine, by the way. This is Zoë, whose work we'll no doubt be seeing."

Zoë smiled dazzlingly at Elaine and said, "Yes, I've got four screenprints over by the sculptures. Have you heard from Charlie recently, by the way? The last I heard, he had his own studio in Cambridge, and was doing frightfully well . . ."

They began to talk about mutual friends and Elaine sipped her wine, watching them, adjusting her impressions of Mark in the light of her closer acquaintance. He seemed altogether more outgoing and sociable than she had imagined from his reticence at the Animal Rights meeting. Watching him chatting and laughing with Zoë, she could see that he exercised a practised charm, his manner subtly flattering. She would be stupid to think that she was singled out for any special attention in that respect, she told herself, disappointed by the realization.

She turned her thoughts to Mark's mention of Sunday – he'd said he would be taking photographs. What was so mysterious and significant about Sundays? She wondered whether Mark would tell her more, if she asked. He'd mentioned it to Zoë casually enough.

"Let me get you some more wine," Mark offered when Zoë had drifted off to join some other friends. Elaine accepted, glad to have his attention again. She was aware that she already felt slightly heady after the first glass, having eaten very little beforehand, but she found the sensation quite pleasant. Mark introduced her to two male acquaintances, his hand resting warm and assured on her shoulder, and she was gratified to notice the distinctly appraising look one of them gave her.

Mark seemed mellowed by these encounters, more disposed to comment favourably on the paintings and sculptures, asking for Elaine's opinion, and appearing to listen quite seriously to what she said. Helped by the wine, she found that she could offer her views with less inhibition than earlier in the evening. She wondered what his own paintings would be like, wishing there were some on display. At least she would know now not to expect washy watercolours.

"These are Laura's – the woman who was at the door," Mark told her, pausing in front of some blodgy paintings in loud colours. Elaine thought they were very clumsy and unrestful and altogether un-expressive, but she kept her thoughts to herself, especially as Laura approached at that moment. Mark made some complimentary remarks about the pictures, and Elaine listened, conscious of a wave of contentment gradually spreading over her, a mixture of the heady effects of the wine, the subtle lighting which seemed to touch everything with glamour, and the sheer pleasure of having Mark, tall and handsome and attentive, beside her. She hoped he would ask her to go out with him again.

"Lovely to see you," Laura told Mark as they left. "I do hope you've enjoyed it," she added politely to Elaine.

"What were you talking about earlier – when you mentioned taking photographs on Sunday?" Elaine asked when they were in the car and speeding homewards.

"Oh, didn't Kate tell you? We're going to break into a veal unit and get some photos to use in our campaign. You can come too, if you like."

Elaine was dumbfounded for a moment. Her thoughts raced. "What do you mean, break in?"

Mark grinned, changing gear with a flourish. "It's quite easy, no damage involved. We just walk into this farm building. They're not locked up, and there won't be anyone around on a Sunday."

Not like breaking and entering, then. Just trespass. Elaine felt perfectly prepared to commit trespass, especially with the double attraction of getting publicity photos and spending more time in Mark's company.

"Thanks. I will come," she replied decisively.

"Fine. I'll pick you up about six o'clock then. I'm picking up Kate and Stuart at a quarter past."

Mark pulled up outside Elaine's house. She wondered whether to invite him in for coffee, but could see from the lighted front window that her parents were in – unusual for them, on a Friday night. A meeting with the parents, she felt, would completely destroy the glamour of the evening.

"Thank you very much for inviting me. I enjoyed it a lot," she said, her words sounding ridiculously formal, she thought, like a prepared speech.

Mark was leaning back in his seat, totally relaxed. She had wondered whether he would kiss her, even a brotherly peck on the cheek (after all, Zoë had kissed him, and that seemed a perfectly normal thing to do). She felt half-relieved, half-disappointed, when he made no move to do anything of the kind, but just said, "OK, see you on Sunday, then."

He drove off as soon as she got out of the car, without looking back. But she didn't care. She thought he was wonderful.

Chapter Four

Kate's face registered surprise and consternation as she opened the front door to see Elaine standing with Mark.

"Oh . . . hello . . ." For once she was at a loss for words.

"Elaine's coming with us," Mark said firmly. "That'll be all right, won't it?"

"Well, it's your car we're going in, so I can hardly object, can I?" Kate said. "Has he told you where we're going?" she added to Elaine.

"Yes."

"Well, as long as you know. I didn't say anything before, because I wasn't sure you'd approve. I thought I might show you the photos afterwards and see how you reacted, then I'd know whether to ask you next time." She was ushering them into the hallway where they received an ecstatic welcome from the bounding mongrel puppy recently adopted from the RSPCA kennels. "Stuart's not here yet," she explained. "I'll make you some tea while we wait."

She showed them into the comfortable clutter of the living room, where her parents were reading the Sunday papers, and a fat black-and-white cat was licking its chest fur with an air of great concentration. Kate's parents were as unlike Elaine's as it was possible to imagine, her mother being exactly like an older and slightly plumper version of Kate, and her father lean and bearded, both of them ageing-hippyish and very easy to get on with.

"Are you in on this too?" they greeted Elaine, obviously fully-informed, and she wondered what it would be like to have parents who could accept their offspring's involvement in such activities without suffering imminent cardiac arrest. All she had said to her own parents was, "I'm going round to Kate's," which was, she told herself, a partial representation of the truth.

Mark had filled her in on the details during the short drive to Kate's house. Stuart apparently shared a flat with someone who had until recently worked as a salesman for an agricultural feed merchant, visiting all the local farms, and this friend had seen the barn with the veal calves in it on one of his visits. Kate, Stuart and Mark had gone on what Mark called "reconnaissance work" the previous Sunday, and had seen the man who presumably looked after the livestock closing up the barn and driving off in a van at about five o'clock. They had checked that the barn wasn't locked up; the door was closed, but only with a heavy wooden latch. "So the idea is," Mark had explained, "for me to take some photos, which we'll try to get in the local paper, or if they won't take them we'll enlarge them to mount on boards and use when we go leafletting." He had seemed tensed-up and alert, eager to get on with it. He wasn't wearing a tie for once, but a brown polo-necked sweater and a dark green jacket. Nothing conspicuous, Elaine thought, glad that she had had the forethought not to dress in startling colours herself.

"Won't Joe be coming?" she asked Kate when she brought in the tray of tea.

"No. We didn't tell him about it. He's on conditional discharge, so he has to stay out of trouble. And there's no point anyway. Mark's the one with the camera, so there's no point in Joe risking it."

Elaine felt shocked, both at the thought of the quiet, mild-mannered Joe being convicted (which he must have been, surely, to get a conditional discharge? Her knowledge of the legal system was hazy) and the way Kate mentioned it so casually in front of her parents. Her own would have had apoplexy. Even Kate's imperturbable mother was looking mildly concerned.

"Risking what?" she enquired, lowering the colour supplement to fix Kate with a stern eye. "I thought you said there was no chance of trouble."

"Oh, there isn't, of course," said Kate hastily, passing her mother a mug of tea. "I meant just in case."

"What was Joe charged with, then?" Mark asked.

"Oh, only breach of the peace and obstruction. It was ridiculous, really. It happened at last year's opening meet. There was a noisy demonstration and some stupid woman rode up to us and her horse shied and she fell off, and blamed it on Joe for waving a banner under its nose. *She* didn't get a conditional discharge, needless to say."

Stuart arrived, and the four of them packed into Mark's Mini. It was almost dark, with a bright half-moon occasionally obscured by hurrying clouds; a cold wind stirred the trees restlessly, bringing leaves whirling across the windscreen. Excitement clutched at Elaine's stomach. Had Mark not been there she knew she would have felt nervous, but with him sitting beside her at the steering wheel, solid and dependable, frowning into the darkness, she felt that she could face anything. She trusted his judgment and experience not to expose them all to unnecessary risks.

"Is it left here, Stuart?" Mark's question reminded her that it was Stuart who had organized the outing, not Mark, and she hardly knew how dependable or otherwise Stuart's judgment was.

"Won't there be a farmhouse or anything, with people in it?" she asked.

"No, it's half-derelict." Stuart spoke quietly, just as confident and assured as Mark. "The farm belongs to the Broadlands Hall Estate. It used to be self-contained, with a tenant farmer. Now the land is farmed by Broadlands Farm – you know, the big farm over towards Alders End.

46

Wheat, mostly. They just use the buildings here, barns and sheds."

"There's a public footpath going right through the farmyard," Kate said, "so if anyone sees us there – not that it's likely in the dark – we've got a perfect excuse."

"Country ramblers," said Mark.

Away from the town, the car headlights illuminated the hedgerows, picking out faded beech leaves and straggling bryony and dried stalks of cow parsley. The lane to the farm was narrow, and there were no other cars about.

"You can park about half a mile further up the lane, past the farm, and we'll walk back," Stuart suggested. "There's a gateway. A bit risky to park any closer, like we did last week."

They piled out, Kate handing Mark his camera from the back seat. It looked a very impressive affair, a Pentax, with various lens attachments and a flash unit.

"Got the torches?" Kate asked Stuart.

"Yes. You carry one and I'll take the other. Keep them off for the moment though, the moon's giving us enough light."

Mark locked up the car and gave Elaine's arm a reassuring squeeze. "Don't worry. Stuart knows what he's doing," he told her quietly.

She smiled back gratefully and followed the others, turning up her coat collar against the sharp wind. They hurried along the deserted lane. The farm buildings stood out, ominous, in stark silhouette against the moonlit sky and the scudding clouds. The blank windows of the derelict farmhouse stared like unwinking eyes, so that Elaine, her imagination fed on half-remembered ghost stories, gave a sudden shiver. Her instincts told her to run away, back to the security of the car, and she knew that she would never dare go into the farmyard if it were not for the comforting presence of the others and the thought of the veal calves waiting in their stalls.

47

A heavy iron gate, padlocked, barred the farm entrance, but a pale stone marked the public footpath, which entered the yard by way of a narrow stile. The ground to the left of the gate sloped down to a pond; Elaine saw the glimmer of water through dark shrubs, and smelled the dankness of pondweed and rotting leaves.

Stuart climbed over the stile and paused cautiously, scanning the quiet buildings. He turned to face them, grinning, his teeth white in the gloom. "No one around. Come on. There's no law against nocturnal footpath exploration."

"Is that where the calves are?" Elaine asked when they were all in the yard. She pointed towards the hulking barn which towered up blackly, beyond the pond.

"No, that's used for storing hay and straw." Stuart pointed at a long low building beyond the farmhouse, about thirty yards from where they were standing. "That's the veal unit. The footpath runs between it and the barn, along a fairly wide track. The entrance to the veal unit is round the back."

They crossed the yard in front of the accusing stare of the black farmhouse windows, stopping in their tracks by a sudden muffled barking and growling.

"Damn!" Mark stood cradling his camera, turning his head towards the sound. "There were no dogs left here last week. The farm bloke took them away with him, two of them."

"Sounds as though they're shut up, over there." Kate nodded in the direction of a small outbuilding at right angles to the veal unit, adjoining a tractor shed.

"D'you think anyone will hear them?" Elaine asked anxiously.

"Shouldn't think so, in this wind. Anyway, they'll surely stop. They must be used to people coming in and out on the footpath." Stuart walked on and the others followed, looking edgily towards the source of the growling and yelping.

Elaine felt exposed, crossing the open farmyard. "What sort of dogs were they?" she whispered to Mark.

"Smallish, terrier sort of jobs. Not Dobermanns or Alsatians," he told her.

They reached the sanctuary of the heavy shadow cast by the towering barn, and Stuart struggled to lift the solid wooden latch of the door. It gave suddenly and the door swung open with a creak.

"Here we are." Stuart stepped inside and switched on his torch, illuminating an oval of straw on the barn floor. Mark followed, and then Elaine and Kate. "Pull the door shut but don't let the latch drop, for God's sake," Stuart told Kate. "I don't fancy spending a night in here."

A sweet warm smell of straw and manure pervaded the air inside the shed. Stuart raised his torch beam, lighting up two surprised eyes in a black-and-white face. Kate switched on her torch, swinging its beam along the rows of stalls. There were startled snuffs and snorts and scufflings as some of the calves tried to scramble to their feet or to run back as far as their limited confines would allow.

Elaine moved closer to the rows of stalls, taking in the details. The pens were no bigger than crates, so narrow that the calves were unable to turn round and would only be able to lie down with their legs folded beneath them. The calves were black-and-white Friesians, apparently from two batches, as some were fluffy babies only just taken from their mothers whilst others were so large that they took up all the available space in their pens. A number was chalked on the wall at the back of each pen. Elaine had seen photographs of veal units before, but nevertheless she was unprepared for the reality of the pathetic creatures with their big flat knees soiled by manure, their pink tongues lolling out of their mouths in search of nourishment, their large eyes rolling, showing the whites. The smell of animal warmth was soothing, at odds with the bleakness of the stalls. She took in the details, the slatted floor which offered no comfort, the bare pens which contained no food, not even water. She remembered that veal calves were often denied water so that they would drink more of the substitute liquid food which was designed to make them put on weight as quickly as possible. Approaching the nearest calf, she tried to stroke its forehead, but it backed away nervously.

"Poor little buggers." Stuart's voice was quiet with compassion and suppressed anger.

"By-products of the dairy industry," said Kate, who never lost the chance of a vegan conversion.

"Oh, if only we could take them away —" Elaine felt helpless. She knew that the crate system of veal production was less widespread than it had once been, many farmers having decided that the method was unnecessarily cruel. But the process was still perfectly legitimate, and she was reminded of the tortuously slow process of government legislation.

"I know, it seems so hopeless just to leave them here," Kate agreed. "But even the RSPCA couldn't do anything about it if we called them. No one's breaking the law."

"Only us," said Mark dryly, consulting a light meter and attaching the flash unit to his camera. "Let's get on. Someone had better wait outside just in case anyone comes."

'I will," Kate offered.

Mark crouched down, looking through his viewfinder, while Stuart moved along the row of stalls selecting the weaker calves and those which looked particularly cramped, so that Mark's photographs would be as emotive as possible. Elaine, keeping out of the way, wandered along the stalls, scratching the calves' necks, looking at their wide frightened eyes and long eyelashes, thinking of cows and calves knee-deep in buttercups in lush June meadows. She knew that Kate was right when she said that these poor creatures were by-products of the dairy industry, for the calves were taken from their mothers so that humans could have the milk. The thought disturbed her; she felt overwhelmed by the enormity of the suffering man inflicted on animals, and the apparent impossibilty of doing anything about it. But, she told herself, if the local paper published the photographs, and people realized what was going on in their own neighbourhood, that might be one small step. You could only take small steps, after all.

The door creaked open. Elaine and the two boys turned in alarm, but it was only Kate. "Elaine, come with me and look at those dogs for a minute," she urged.

"OK." Elaine was half-glad to leave the sad calves, with their reproachful eyes. Outside, the cold wind tugged at her jacket and sent an icy blast down her neck.

"They're locked up in a sort of kennel." Kate led the way purposefully across the yard, past the dark shed where the tractor with its high cockpit waited like an aeroplane in its hangar, surrounded by various bits of rusting machinery. At the end of the tractor shed was a wooden lean-to building with a low door, and windows covered in wire mesh.

"There must be at least three in there. Don't let them out," Elaine warned. The dogs might not be Alsatians or Dobermanns, but terriers could be fierce enough.

"It's all right. They're in cages inside. I looked through the window with my torch." Kate gave the door a firm tug and it opened to reveal a dark, uninviting interior. Elaine, trying to banish thoughts of spiders and rats, followed Kate inside. The torch beam revealed three cages: the first was empty, and the second and third contained a pair of wire-haired terriers and a pair of Jack Russells. One of the Jack Russells flung itself at the wire of its cage in a fury of barking, and the other three dogs growled menacingly, showing their teeth.

Elaine grabbed Kate's arm. "Shine your torch in that empty cage for a minute. There's something in there."

The object she had seen proved to be a leather muzzle,

lying discarded beside an empty water bowl, and the two girls stared at each other for a moment, taking in the implication that there might be another dog, a ferocious guard dog perhaps, at large on the farm.

"Surely not," said Kate, acknowledging the unspoken thought. "It would have put in an appearance by now, especially after the others barked when we arrived."

"It's a pretty large muzzle. Too big for one of these small dogs."

"Yes." Kate considered the muzzle thoughtfully for a moment, then turned her torchbeam back on the Jack Russells. "I wonder if these are hunt terriers. Look at this one's scarred nose and torn ear."

"You mean, they're used for going down earths after foxes?"

"It seems likely, doesn't it? They're obviously not pets, kept in a shed like this, and there aren't any cows or sheep which might account for them being working dogs . . ."

"*Kate*!" Elaine grabbed Kate's arm again, more urgently this time, as a beam of light from outside swung round and shone through the open door. At the same moment, the wind dropped and they heard the clank of the chain by the main gate, and a car engine running.

"Christ!" The whites of Kate's eyes were very bright in the gloom. The car pulled forward so that the lights shone towards the hay barn, and the two girls peeping cautiously out of the door, could see a man re-padlocking the gate.

"There are at least two of them," Kate whispered in despair. "If they catch Mark taking photos, we're done for."

They shrank back into the shadows. "Listen," Kate muttered rapidly. "They'll have seen the door open here, so they're bound to come over and check. You rush round and try to warn the others – I'll distract them, pretending to be lost or something."

Elaine's heart was pounding wildly. A glance confirmed

52

that the man at the gate was out of sight, blocked from view by a corner of the farmhouse, while the driver of the van was parking it next to the hay barn. Keeping to the grassy edge of the yard for quietness' sake, she hared along the front edge of the veal unit and darted round to the back door. Thank God they had left the door open. She slipped in silently. Mark and Stuart, engrossed in photography, were still kneeling in the straw.

"Quick," she hissed, "there are two men in the yard. Get away down the footpath before they see you. We'll meet you back at the car."

The two boys wasted no time asking questions. Mark scooped up his camera accessories and within seconds they were out of the door and vanishing into the darkness. Elaine followed them, closed the door carefully and tried to control her shaking legs and rapid breathing enough to walk round into the yard to help Kate face the two men. She hoped Kate had had time to think of a plausible story.

Kate had apparently decided that a bold approach would be most convincing. She was walking towards the van, shining her torch at the ground in front of her.

"Who the hell are you?" The man who had been driving turned to face her abruptly, his voice harsh, and Elaine took advantage of his distraction to swerve in her course so that she appeared to come from the same direction as Kate. Another dog, with a deeper, more ominous bark, could be heard inside the van, and she hoped the men weren't planning to let it out just yet.

"I'm terribly sorry to trouble you at this time of the evening." Kate's voice was transformed by a quite uncharacteristic politeness. "You see, we've lost our dog. He ran away from us earlier this afternoon, and we thought he might be around here because we often walk through on this footpath."

The second man, shorter and stockier than the first, came round the footpath from the house and eyed the two girls. Elaine, glancing at Kate's attire, noted with infinite relief that her friend had had the forethought to dress innocuously in a black jacket quite unadorned by badges. A single Animal Rights slogan would have given the game away immediately, but there was nothing about Kate to suggest that she was anything other than a distraught dog-lover.

"We're terribly anxious," Kate continued. "You see, he's not much more than a puppy, and he's never run away from home before. And now that it's dark, he must be so frightened . . ."

Elaine, impressed by this accomplished performance, contributed, "Yes, poor little Benjie," trying to inject just the right amount of highly-strung female dottiness into her voice.

Both men were middle-aged, dressed in dark green waterproof coats. They scrutinized the girls suspiciously, while the dog in the van continued to bark and growl. The taller man, who had thin craggy features and wore a flat cloth cap, said, "You were over by the kennels just now, weren't you?"

"Yes," Kate agreed. "We heard the dogs barking and I thought Benjie might have been attracted by the other dogs, or someone might even have found him and shut him in for safe keeping until the morning."

The shorter man was looking at Kate belligerently. "The footpath runs along this side of the yard, by the pond, not over there," he said accusingly.

Kate gave him a sweet smile. "Yes, but I'm sure you won't mind, under the circumstances. We don't normally wander off the footpath, of course."

"We're terribly sorry," Elaine put in with an apologetic simper.

The taller man looked from Kate to Elaine and back again, evidently decided that they were harmless females rather than trespassers bent on vandalism, and said, "Hm,

54

well, we'll keep an eye out for your dog. What does he look like?"

"A black cocker spaniel, with a few white hairs on his chest, ten months old, wearing a green leather collar," Kate replied promptly. "Perhaps you could give me a ring if you do see him, if it's not too much trouble. My name's Elizabeth French, Alders End 791."

"Elizabeth French, Alders End 791," repeated the man. "Right. We'll let you know."

"Thank you *so* much," Kate gushed with a benevolent smile like a countess at a garden party.

"Thank you," Elaine echoed. "Good night."

They left the yard by the stile, conscious that the men continued watching until they were off the premises.

"You were terrific," Elaine said admiringly as soon as they were out of earshot. "The headmaster would have you making speeches to the governors if he knew just how polite you could be."

The boys were waiting at the van, with the engine running. Stuart sprang out as he saw the girls coming. "What happened? Did they suspect anything?"

"We thought they must have invited you in for a cup of tea and a chat, you've been so long," Mark remarked casually.

"I like that. We've been face to face with the enemy, hairsbreadth scapes in the imminent deadly breach and all that, while you've been calmly sitting here," Kate retorted.

"Anyway, we got away with it," Elaine reported with satisfaction. "Thanks to Elizabeth French."

The boys exchanged puzzled glances and Mark said, "Who the hell's Elizabeth French?"

By the time they had exchanged news, Mark confirming that he thought he had taken sufficient photographs for their purposes, the Mini was racing along the country lanes towards the town, buffeted by occasional gusts of high wind. The girls' feeling of relief, after the farmyard encounter, was infectious; no one felt that it would be a suitable end to the evening simply to go tamely to their respective homes.

"I'm starving," Mark said, taking a bend rather fast, so that Elaine was thrown against Kate in the back seat. "Anyone feel like an Indian takeaway? We could go round to my place."

"Sounds OK to me. What about you two? Anyone got any money?" Stuart asked, searching in his jacket pockets. Everyone dug out what cash they had and Stuart added up the pooled resources. "Yes, I think we might just about have enough. Where are you going, Mark? *The Star of the Punjab*, or whatever it's called?"

"Is that the one by the cinema?"

"Tell you what, Stuart." Kate leaned forward, suddenly animated by a new idea. "If we let Elaine and Mark go in and choose the food, we could take a little stroll along to the butcher's and put some stickers on the windows. I've got some in my pocket."

"Good idea," Stuart approved. "Sunday night's a good time for that."

Elaine had seen Kate's stickers, small squares with the message: "Warning – cruelty to animals", which she carried around with her at all times to stick on menus, cuts of meats on supermarket shelves, and fur coats worn by women in front of her in queues.

"What is it then – Tandoori chicken for everyone?" Mark asked, locking up the car.

Kate put on a schoolmarmish expression. "Elaine, you're responsible for making sure we get edible food. Come on, Stuart. See you two back here."

The atmosphere inside the Indian restaurant was dark and spicy and intimate. Looking at the takeaway menu, Elaine wished that she and Mark were going to sit down together, looking at each other in the candlelight, their knees touching under the table. She glanced at his inscrutable profile as he studied the menu; he appeared unmoved by the evening's events. He was difficult to get to know, she thought, every bit as diffident and enigmatic as she had supposed at first. She was intrigued by the proposed visit to "his place", feeling that an inside view of his home must provide more insight into his character than her acquaintance with him so far had done. It occurred to her that she didn't know where he lived, whether it was with his parents or alone. She couldn't imagine him living with his parents; he was far too independent. She wondered whether he would ask her to go out with him again, somewhere romantic this time, she hoped, where they could talk and she could have his whole attention . . .

"Do you like onion bhajis?"

"Oh . . . er . . .yes." She felt herself colouring up, as if what she had been thinking was written on her face. She turned her attention to the menu.

Mark's place proved to be a first-floor flat in a spacious and rather dilapidated Victorian house. He shared it, Elaine gathered, with someone called Robin, who was a student at the art college. "He's out this evening, though," Mark said, showing them into a large, high-ceilinged room, while he went into the kitchen for plates and forks. Elaine, settling on a big floor cushion, looked around with interest. There were dozens of books, overflowing the inadequate shelves and piled up on the floor, lots of art books, and some with learned names like *The Etruscan Empire* and *The Dawn of Romanticism*. There were several canvases leaning against the wall, face down, unfortunately, and one painting on the wall above the fireplace, showing a dead, gnarled tree in a desolate landscape, executed in rich, earthy colours. Elaine wondered if it were Mark's, and thought of the drawing he had done of herself. She hoped he had kept it, not torn it up and thrown it away.

Mark brought in the food on a tray, with glasses of water,

and they all knelt on the floor to heap up their plates. Kate was talking about the opening meet, the next important item in the Animal Rights calendar.

"You are all coming, aren't you? We could do with you and your camera, Mark."

"Yes, count me in. I love the thrill of the chase." Mark smiled in his usual faintly sardonic way, as if amused at some private joke.

He got out some bottles of beer and cider after the meal, and they sat chatting companionably for a while. Elaine said little, leaning back against the wall with her glass of cider in her hand. Her mind wandered over the events of the evening, picturing the rows of calves in the darkness, the dogs locked in their bleak cages, the empty muzzle . . . She felt suddenly overcome by weariness, an accumulation of the tension and the spicy food and the cider, her eyelids almost dropping. She wondered what would happen when it was time to leave. Perhaps Mark would drive her home, and perhaps he'd suggest another outing, just the two of them . . .

Stuart was yawning and stretching and saying, "Well, I guess it's time to hit the road. Some of us have jobs to go to in the morning."

Mark got to his feet. "I'll come down with you. I'll take you home, Elaine."

"Oh, I can easily drop Elaine off," Stuart offered. "My car's just round the corner, at Kate's, and it's not far out of my way. Save you going out again."

Mark's face expressed no particular regret. He shrugged noncommittally. "OK, if you're going that way. I'll see you next week about the negatives, Kate. See you, Stuart. Bye, Elaine."

Elaine followed Kate and Stuart down the stairs. The brightness had abruptly faded from the evening; she felt crushed with disappointment.

Chapter Five

"Well, I did think you'd receive the idea with a little more enthusiasm." Mr Parsonage slumped in his chair, his whole demeanour expressing gloom from his unkempt dark hair down to his scuffed suede shoes. "You are supposed to be literary devotees, after all."

"We haven't got time for frivolities like plays," protested one of the boys. "It's bad enough trying to keep up with the usual work without having to learn enormous great speeches and prance round in tights, like a load of poofters."

"Why does it have to be a Shakespeare play?" Kate queried. "They're all so *long*. And difficult to learn."

There were murmurs of agreement, and Mr Parsonage explained drearily, "The headmaster particularly wants it – this joint do with the girls' school. And they've always done a Shakespeare play. It's traditional."

"It's never too late for a break with tradition," someone muttered into the doleful silence which followed. The younger Dodds Green pupils seldom encountered the girls from the grammar school, other than to exchange taunts on the buses, generally considering them to be a snooty lot. Now, as sixth formers, they were suddenly expected not only to be civil but to throw themselves wholeheartedly into a production of *As You Like It*.

"It's such a stupid story," complained a boy called Paul, "girls dressing up as boys and dozens of people skulking about in a forest."

"They're providing Rosalind. They've got a star pupil who wants to go on to drama school," said Mr Parsonage. "So that's the main part taken care of. They'll probably provide all the female parts, in fact."

"Great! Did you hear that?" Kate turned round to Elaine, Ann and an Indian girl called Sita, the other girls in the group. "They don't want us at all – this joint production is just a devious way of getting their hands on our boys. Can we go and get on with our work now?" she asked Mr Parsonage pointedly.

"Not so fast. I don't get the impression the boys are exactly falling over themselves to join the cast." Mr Parsonage looked critically at the boys, who were mostly avoiding catching his eye. "There's no reason why girls shouldn't take some of the male parts. I've already found someone to play Orlando – David Easton in the upper sixth, who's very keen, unlike you lot – but there are lots of smaller parts to fill. And we shall want people to paint the scenery. Elaine, you're doing art, aren't you?"

"Yes," said Elaine.

"Well, Mr Rose will be speaking to you about that, no doubt."

"You'd better get cracking," Kate said dryly. "The Forest of Arden in glorious technicolour."

Mr Parsonage sighed heavily and began collecting together the papers on his desk, signifying that the meeting was at an end. "Give it some thought, all of you. You'd probably *enjoy* it, once you committed yourselves." He looked round at the sceptical group, without much optimism. "There's to be a meeting of all those wanting to take part, the first day back after half term. I'll be approaching people individually in the meantime." He stood up to go. "And don't forget those Lawrence essays will be due in the same day," he added as a parting shot.

"What a cheek." Paul lolled back in his chair, swung his feet up on to the table in front and began flicking tiny pellets of paper towards the wastepaper bin. "'Approaching people individually' – press ganging, he means."

"Learn the lines, paint the scenery, make the costumes,

60

no doubt," said Ann. "'Oh, and don't forget to hand in your essays on time.'"

Elaine joined in the general moaning, but secretly rather liked the idea of seeing Shakespeare's play brought to life, even if it was only David Easton and the others in tights. It might be fun to have a smal', not-too-demanding part, she thought, and to paint the scenery. When Mr Rose collared her later, she agreed to go to the meeting. By that time, Ann and Sita and Paul and even Kate had been persuaded that they should take on minor roles in the interests of furthering their insight into the workings of Shakespeare's theatre.

Meanwhile, Elaine had more pressing thoughts on her mind. She hadn't seen Mark at school, and now it was the last day before the half term break. The only definite arrangement for seeing him was at the opening meet on Saturday week, and that was far too long to wait. The empty days of the holiday seemed to stretch ahead stultifyingly. Perhaps Mark might ring her. She stayed at home that evening, reading, her ears straining for the telephone. When it did ring, she let her father go to answer it, waiting in the lounge with her heart thumping. But her father's, "Oh, hello Harry, how are you?" sent her spirits thudding down to floor level.

"What's the matter with you, Elaine? You look all on edge," her father remarked, returning to the lounge.

"Oh, nothing." But she couldn't prevent the disappointment from showing in her voice.

She was behaving in a totally ridiculous way, she told herself impatiently. Mark obviously hadn't intended the art exhibition evening to be any more than a one-off. He hadn't implied anything to make her think otherwise. He probably hadn't given her a thought since Sunday.

She wondered whether she could approach him and suggest going somewhere. There were no rules about it, were there? From glossy magazines, she knew that it was perfectly acceptable for girls to ask men out – indeed, that it was rather fashionable to do so. But this emancipated picture didn't quite square up to real life, when she considered people she knew at school; the boys did the asking, while the girls merely lured them with coy smiles and fluttering eyelashes. It was the fear of being turned down that was so off-putting; she felt that she could brace herself and ask Mark to go out with her if only she could be certain he would accept. There was really nothing to lose, she told herself; if he did refuse, she would at least know for sure that he wasn't interested. But how to actually put it into practice was less easy to decide. She rehearsed several nonchalant-sounding openings, rejecting each one as soon as she thought of it.

The idea struck her when she was lying in bed next morning. Now that she knew where Mark's flat was, she could easily call in, in the early evening, and pretend that she was just passing, and ask him how he was getting on with the veal unit photographs. In fact she already knew, because Kate had told her that he had taken them into the local newspaper office together with an article she had written, but she could pretend ignorance. Then, when they had discussed the photographs, she could casually – as if the idea had just occurred to her – suggest that they went out somewhere. There would be nothing outrageous about that.

By the time she was walking along the road where Mark lived, the idea seemed less good, and she almost wavered and turned back. But, spurred on by the thought of more evenings by the silent telephone, she marched boldly up the front path and rang the doorbell. After a moment, she heard someone running downstairs.

"Hi." A thin young man with lank fair hair, dressed in a paint-stained sweater and cords, was looking at her blankly. Music drifted down from the floor above, something classical-sounding.

"Hi." She tried to sound just as casual. "Is Mark in?"

"Yes, he's upstairs. Mark!" the young man bellowed up the stairs. "Someone to see you." He gestured to her to come in, and she followed him up the stairs. This must be Robin, the art student. She'd forgotten that he might be there. A smell of cooking food wafted out as they passed the kitchen door. Perhaps she'd mis-timed her visit. They might be about to eat.

Robin showed her into the sitting room, where Mark sat on a low stool with a drawing board on his knees and several large books strewn on the floor in front of him. He looked up as she entered, and his face broke into a smile of what seemed to be genuine pleasure. He put down his drawing board and stood up.

"Elaine! Have you come about the scenery?"

Elaine, completely thrown by his question, stared at him idiotically. "The what?"

"The scenery." He waved a hand towards his drawing board. "For the play. *As You Like It*," he continued, as her expression remained blank.

"Oh, I *see*." Elaine didn't see, but as she spoke she realized that a new opportunity for casual visits had presented itself without her knowledge. "How did you get roped in for that?"

Mark sat down again and picked up the drawing he'd been working on, gesturing to her to sit down on the sofa. "Parsonage asked me. He asked if I'd like an acting part, but I said I'd rather take care of the scenery. He said you might help out. What do you think of this?" He passed her the drawing, looking rather pleased with himself.

Elaine studied it, slightly needled by his assumption that he'd be taking care of the scenery and she merely helping, but mollified by the thought of all the hours they would need to spend together before the scenery would be perfected. With one glance she could tell that Mark's proposed backcloth was infinitely superior to anything conjured up by her dull imagination and unskilled hand. It was what she thought of as a William Morris-like scene, woodland, with some parts vaguely sketched in and others executed in detail. The trees were elegant and stylized, forming a leafy canopy over slender, aesthetically-placed trunks, with arching stems of bluebells dotting the ground between them. Elaine realized that what she had pictured in her mind would definitely come into the category of washy watercolour.

"It's lovely," she said lamely.

"I thought perhaps something in bold black-and-white for Act One, the court scenes. Then we'll need to see what kind of lighting's available. For the forest scenes we'll need pale blue lighting, if they've got it, for a daylight effect."

"Have you done this sort of thing before, then?" Elaine asked. It hadn't occurred to her even to consider the lighting.

Mark took the drawing back and scrutinized it critically. "Yes. I did a few things with the Youth Theatre where I used to live. A bit of acting and some set design."

Elaine looked at him, awed. Was there anything he *couldn't* do? Painting, photography, acting, set designing . . . no wonder he wasn't interested in her, so gauche and inexperienced.

"Why did you come round, then, if it wasn't about the play?" He turned to face her, his glance shrewd and direct, and she felt herself flushing, remembering her ploy.

"Oh – I was just passing and I wondered how you'd got on with the photos . . ." she began.

Mark gave one of his inscrutable grins and she wondered whether he had guessed the real reason. "Stuart and I took them round to the *Gazette*, but they didn't know if they'd use them. Said they might put them in the free local paper, though."

64

"That would be something," Elaine said. "The free paper probably has more readers than the *Gazette*."

"Yes. Anyway, I'll do the enlargements and we can use them ourselves, as well. I haven't done any of the prints yet, only the ones I gave the paper, or I'd show them to you. Are you doing anything in particular this evening? I was just thinking, if you're not, we could go to the cinema. *The Inner Circle*'s showing."

Elaine could hardly believe her luck. The invitation had been issued casually enough – there was nothing to suggest that Mark had gone through such inner agonies as she had – but nevertheless it was a definite invitation. She could forget her rehearsed lines of studied nonchalance.

"Oh, that would be nice. I hadn't planned to do anything else." She hesitated, hearing the sound of clattering saucepan lids from the kitchen. "But aren't you just about to eat? It's quite early . . ."

"Yes, Robin's cooking something. Would you like to have some? I don't know what it is. His meals are fairly unpredictable – he just throws in whatever's lying around. Or have you got to go home to eat?"

"No," Elaine countered hastily. "But I'm not hungry, thank you. I had something to eat earlier."

Mark looked at his watch. "Well, if you don't mind waiting while I stuff myself, we could go straight after that. I'll check the time the film starts. I've got a local paper somewhere."

He found the paper and then introduced her rather belatedly to Robin. "He does have some rather primitive habits, but I'm doing my best to civilize him. He's turning into quite a respectable cook."

"Thanks," said Robin dryly. "Glad to be of use."

The two boys ate their meal on trays on their laps, while Elaine accepted a cup of tea and an apple. She liked the comfortable informal domesticity of the thrown-together meal, the room softly lit by reading lamps, and the warm glow of the gas fire. Like Kate's house, it made her realize how very un-cosy her own home was, with its immaculately hoovered and dusted and polished rooms, so that if you left a book lying on a chair you immediately felt you had spoiled the perfection. Thinking of home brought to her the realization that she ought to let her parents know where she was. They hadn't been in when she'd left, and she hadn't said anything, feeling superstitiously certain that her plan would fail if she did.

"Have you got a telephone?" she asked Mark, who was stacking the plates. "I ought to phone home and tell them I'll be late back."

"Downstairs in the hall."

It was her mother who answered, not her father as she had hoped; he would be less inquisitive.

"To the cinema?" Her mother's voice was so strident that she feared Mark would hear it upstairs. "With Alistair, do you mean? Where are you?"

"No, not with Alistair. With someone else. Mark, someone from school."

"Why didn't you mention it before?"

"I didn't know I was going. I . . . bumped into him."

"How will you get home? You know the buses aren't reliable late at night, and I don't like you wandering about on your own in the dark."

"It's all right. Mark's got a car."

"Who is this Mark? Do I know of him?"

"I'll tell you tomorrow. Bye then. I won't be late back." She put the receiver down before her mother could ask for a written character reference.

Upstairs, Mark had put on a tie and his suede jacket, and was combing his hair in front of a mirror in the upstairs hall.

"Oh, you look lovely, dearie," Robin told Mark in effeminate tones, passing through with the plates on a tray.

66

"I know," Mark replied quite seriously.

"Well, don't keep the lady waiting."

It was dark outside and Elaine remembered that at the weekend the clocks would be going back for winter, making it dark by five o'clock. The thought brought with it associations of Christmas, walks in the snow and evenings indoors reading. And, she hoped, evenings like this, setting out with Mark.

"I'm glad you came round," Mark said in the car, negotiating a roundabout. "I was going to be away for a few days, visiting my parents. Otherwise I would have suggested going out somewhere. But then I couldn't get the time off work, so now I'm going to spend the weekend with them, and a few days of next week. I'm leaving tomorrow night."

He turned to look at her as he finished speaking, and she felt that he must be able to see the great flood of joy that rushed into her face. His few words seemed to alter the status of their relationship, elevating it to one in which she could reasonably expect him to keep her informed of his plans. It was disappointing that he would be going away, of course, but that was a minor setback.

"Oh, that's all right," she managed to say in a fairly normal voice. "Where do your parents live?"

"In Hampshire. I used to live there too, until a couple of years ago. Then I came up here, to go to art school. But I didn't stick it. I prefer to do things my own way. That's why I decided to take the job at the bank – have time for painting on my own, and earn a bit of money as well."

Elaine wondered what his parents were like, and what they thought of him abandoning art school and his subsequent independent attitude. She couldn't imagine her own parents tolerating such waywardness. But then Mark was a good few years older than she was, old enough to do exactly as he liked.

Afterwards, she could only remember the plot of the

film in a confused blur. It was a political thriller, fast-paced with terse dialogue, so that she found it hard to keep track of the double-dealings and mistaken identities. But she remembered very clearly that at one point Mark had leaned towards her and whispered, "Confusing, isn't it?" and his arm had crept round her shoulders and stayed there, with his hand just touching her ear; and leaving the cinema he had taken her hand, his clasp warm and reassuring. And when they pulled up in the car outside her house, he had said, "I enjoyed tonight," and moved so close that she was aware of his clean, slightly astringent aftershave smell, and very gently kissed her. She floated indoors in a haze of euphoria, feeling as heady as if she'd been drinking champagne.

The next morning she awoke with a delicious remembrance of the evening, coupled with gloom because Mark would be going away for a few days. It was a quite new experience for her, this feeling of almost desperate dependence on someone else. She had been out with other boys before, but that had been casual, for fun, not occupying her thoughts at all between times. This was completely different, the feeling that her whole life was in suspension. I love him, she told herself. The thought that he might ever love her in return seemed impossible, filling her with despair, the combination of joy and hopelessness resolving itself into an almost physical ache somewhere in the pit of her stomach.

"What on earth's the matter with you?" Kate asked, calling round in the late afternoon. "You don't look quite all there."

"Oh . . . nothing. I've been working hard." Elaine had intended to spend the day usefully, getting up to date with her reading and essays, so that she could have the rest of the half term break free. But she had found it impossible to concentrate, and had wasted much time staring at a page of notes, taking in nothing at all.

"Did you enjoy the film last night?" Kate was studying her shrewdly. "I saw you coming out. I went with Stuart."

"Oh –" Elaine went scarlet, remembering coming out into the sharp cold air, holding Mark's hand. She wouldn't have noticed Kate if she had been standing in front of her.

"Got it pretty bad, old girl, haven't you?" Kate said, not unsympathetically. "Well, he's going home for a few days, isn't he, so shake yourself out of it and come and do some leafletting tomorrow. Which reminds me – I came to show you this, in case you hadn't got yours yet."

She flourished a newspaper and unfolded it on the table, smoothing out the pages. "Centre pages – look. We're in."

Elaine looked. There were three of Mark's photographs, one showing the whole interior of the veal unit, the other two showing individual calves and the cramped dimensions of their pens. The article was headed *The Price of Veal*, and described the conditions graphically. Nowhere was the name of the farm mentioned; the implication was that the pictures were representative of veal units concealed from the public all over the country, and Kate's article made it clear that thousand of calves exported from Britain were destined for such units on the Continent.

"Not bad, eh? I never thought we'd get such a spread," said Kate approvingly. "Perhaps just one photo in a corner somewhere was all I hoped for."

"It's wonderful," Elaine agreed. "And it's a very good article, Kate. That should make people think. Leafletting tomorrow, did you say?"

"Yes. I've got the veal leaflets. It'll be a good follow-up as lots of people will have seen the free paper. We could stand outside the supermarket, I thought, where they sell veal."

Kate's choice of venue did not seem such a good idea when, soon after they had started, a policeman came ominously towards them and told them that they couldn't hand out leaflets at the supermarket front without permission from the manager. "You can carry on, but go and stand in the main precinct where you won't be obstructing or upsetting anyone," he advised.

Kate gave him a leaflet, and grudgingly moved away from her position in front of the Meat Marketing Board poster on the supermarket window, returning to leave a few of her stickers on it when the policeman had gone. On the credit side, several people stopped to say that they had seen the newspaper article and thought it was terrible, and some said that they wouldn't buy veal again, or eat it in restaurants.

"That's something, I suppose," Elaine said as they walked away from the precinct at closing time. "A small step for vealkind, even if we couldn't actually do anything for those poor calves."

"I know. It makes you feel so frustrated." Kate paused to direct the filthiest possible stare at a passing woman in a fur coat. "You can understand people like Terry wanting to actually rescue animals from slaughter."

"Yes," Elaine agreed. "It's difficult, though – I mean, what do you do with the animals once you've rescued them?"

"That is the problem. It's not easy to hide twenty veal calves in your back garden. Especially when they grow up to be bulls."

Shortly after Elaine arrived home, there was a ring at the door bell. Reminding herself that it couldn't possibly be Mark, she opened the door to find Alistair.

"Oh, you're in. I thought I saw you walking past the window just now."

"Yes, I've been into town. Come in."

He followed her into the kitchen and sat down on a stool. She had known him for so long that everything about him was familiar, from the way his fringe always flopped into his eyes to the Aran sweater he wore.

"I haven't seen you for ages," he told her reproachfully. "Have you been busy?"

"Yes, I suppose I have really. Would you like some tea?"

"Yes, please. Are you involved in this Shakespeare do at school?"

"Only doing the scenery, and perhaps a very small part. Are you in it, then?"

"Yes. I'm one of those Lords who wanders about in the woods – Amiable, or something."

"Amiens, you mean."

"That's it. They roped me in for that because I can play the flute. And I've actually got to *sing*, can you believe it? Everyone'll be in hysterics."

Elaine reached into the refrigerator for the milk jug. "I don't suppose you'll be the only person making a fool of yourself. Some of the things people have got to say to each other . . ."

"I know." They smiled at each other, slipping back into their old easy-going companionship. "Actually, what I came round for," Alistair continued, "is to see whether you felt like going to the pictures tonight. There's that spy thriller on, *The Inner Circle*."

"Oh – " Elaine hesitated. "I've already seen it," she said awkwardly.

Alistair's face dropped. "Have you? Who did you go with?"

If he hadn't looked so miserable, she would have been tempted to tell him to mind his own business. But better to get it over with, she decided. "I went with Mark Harrington, you know, who does English."

Alistair looked at her sadly for a moment, then dropped his gaze to study his shoes. "Are you going out with him, then? Regularly, I mean?"

"I don't know . . . I mean . . . I've only seen him a few times." Why should she feel so guilty, for heaven's sake, she asked herself angrily. She hadn't promised herself to Alistair, had she?

There was a silence so pronounced that the kitchen clock could be heard ticking. Then Alistair looked up at her with something like anguish. "But I thought we . . . I thought you and I . . ." His voice was not quite steady. "I never thought you'd go out with anybody else," he finished reproachfully.

She stared back, aghast at his obvious distress. "But I . . . I mean, we're just friends, we've never . . ." She searched for the words to tell Alistair kindly that she couldn't begin to feel for him a fraction of what she felt for Mark, that he could never be more than someone kind and comfortable to have around. But there were no tactful words to frame such thoughts. "I didn't know you expected us to be any more than friends," she finished lamely.

"Is that it, then? You'd rather go out with him?"

"Yes," she whispered, seeing no alternative to telling the truth.

Alistair sighed heavily and stood up. "Well, I might as well go, then. Don't bother about the tea."

He walked to the front door. She followed him blindly to the front door, not knowing what to say, but desperately wanting to say something to restore their old friendship. "Alistair, don't go yet. We can still be friends, can't we?"

"It won't be the same any more." He turned to face her. "I just hope you know what you're doing, Elaine, for your own good. I like you enough not to want you to get hurt."

She stared after him as he strode down the front path without looking back.

Chapter Six

"Right. We'll try to get the complete cast list drawn up by tomorrow, then," Mr Parsonage said decisively. "And you'll be bringing the girls over to start rehearsing on Monday."

He directed the final part of his remark towards a grey-haired, fierce-looking female teacher who, throughout the meeting, had been giving superior, disparaging glances at the Dodds Green pupils. Mr Parsonage looked rather fraught, and kept pushing his hands through his dark wavy hair, a sure sign of agitation, with the result that a large unruly tuft of it was now sticking out at right angles to his head. This, combined with the fact that he had sat on some chalk and now had white dust smudged half over the seat of his trousers, made him look like a caricature of a distraught schoolmaster.

In contrast, the grammar school girls looked quite calm about the whole affair. Caroline Radway, who had been introduced as the girl who was to play Rosalind, drew appreciative glances from all the boys present. She was tall and slender, both these necessary attributes for the role she was to play, with fair hair cut very short in a flattering boyish style which accentuated her delicate features and wide, hazel eyes. David Easton, Elaine noticed, was looking decidedly cheered by the prospect of playing her lover, Orlando.

"And you're taking care of the scenery?" The grey-haired teacher had an abrasive voice to match her face.

"Yes, Mark Harrington's in charge of that." Mr Parsonage scanned the faces. "Oh, he's not here, is he? It's not one of his days in."

"Elaine's doing the scenery," Kate pointed out sharply.

"Oh yes, Mark told me he'd arranged one or two helpers," Mr Parsonage replied dismissively. "And some of the other Adult Education students have kindly offered to help with lighting and costumes."

Elaine was glad that Mark wasn't at the meeting, because of Alistair's presence. She knew it was inevitable that they would all three meet, sooner or later, at rehearsals, but felt that she wasn't up to handling such a situation just yet, with her emotions in their current state of confusion. She rather hoped that Mark would get on with his scenery and stay in the background. However, these hopes were dashed when Mr Parsonage returned to his cast list, and said, "Well, I can't see who we can get to play Jacques, unless I can persuade Mark to do it. There's nobody else left who's up to it."

"Mark has had some acting experience," Miss Blackburn, the other English teacher, agreed.

Elaine's heart sank. Jacques and Amiens were both Lords attending Duke Senior, which meant that, if Mark agreed, he and Alistair would be involved in the same scenes. It didn't make for an easy situation. But she checked herself swiftly, telling herself that she was probably giving the matter far more importance than either of the two boys.

Over the half term break she had had plenty of opportunity to brood, her longing to see Mark again confused with her uneasiness over the break with Alistair. She wondered what would have happened if she hadn't met Mark. She supposed it would have been easy to drift on with Alistair, becoming increasingly dependent on him for company, drifting eventually as far as an engagement, perhaps, and even marriage. Many marriages must come about in that way, because even if you secretly yearned for something more exciting and dramatic, it was easier to carry on than to make the decision to break off with someone you were, after all, fond of. She thought of married people she knew, her own parents, for instance, or their many friends. It was hard to imagine any of them falling in love with each other, experiencing the turmoil of happiness and doubt and despair which the mere mention of Mark's name could provoke in her. Yet, no matter how great the unhappiness which she knew was in Mark's power to give her, she felt it infinitely preferable to the plodding security of a relationship with Alistair.

"That girl – Caroline whatsit," Kate said as they left school in the early dusk. "I've seen her before somewhere. I can't think where, though."

"Isn't she attractive?" Elaine remarked enviously. "She looks like a model or something."

"All right, I suppose." Kate never paid much attention to appearances, her own or other people's. "Looks right for Rosalind, anyway. But how they're going to make you look like Adam, I can't imagine."

Elaine giggled. "A false beard, I suppose, and make-up to make me look ancient. At least it's a nice small part, not like yours."

"I know." Kate had been persuaded into the fairly substantial part of Touchstone, the fool. "After they *promised* we could get away with a nice little walk-on bit here and there. I've got so much to say, I'd better go home and start learning it straight away. And Dad's giving me a driving lesson tonight." Kate had recently had her seventeenth birthday and was determined to be the first of the lower sixth to pass her driving test.

Elaine had almost been counting the hours until she could reasonably expect Mark to phone her. The call, when it came, was disappointing – he was staying on an extra day at his parents', because of sudden car trouble, which he wanted to get fixed before attempting the return journey. "So I won't see you until Saturday, the opening meet," he concluded. "We can all go together, Kate and

Stuart and you and me. I'll pick you up about nine-fifteen."

Elaine, shattered with disappointment because she would have to wait at least another thirty-six hours to see him, and then only in the company of others, rang Kate for consolation, if not actual sympathy. Kate was not the type to encourage emotional outpourings, but took, as usual, a brisk, practical approach. "Come round tomorrow night straight from school and we can make a big banner to take on Saturday. No point sitting at home moping."

Kate's mother provided an unwanted white sheet, and Kate had thought of a slogan, "BAN BLOOD SPORTS – GIVE HUNTING THE BOOT", to be executed in large red letters. "If there's time we can do a picture, too," she suggested. "Or rather you can do it – you're the artistic one."

It was rather a time-consuming business, with poster paints spread out on the dining room table, but at last it was finished, including the illustration of which Elaine felt rather proud. She had painted a huge spurred riding boot, kicking a miniature figure in hunting dress off the edge of the banner. The figure was a tiny fat man, with a handlebar moustache, and a bulging stomach straining at the buttons of his scarlet coat, and she had managed to get just the right expression of indignant outrage into his pop eyes.

"Brilliant!" Kate approved, sewing rough seams at each side through which poles could be inserted. It would look quite eye-catching, Elaine thought, imagining the reactions of the hunting people. "What do they usually do when demonstrators turn up?" she asked.

"Depends what happens. Mostly, at the meet, they just ignore us and make supercilious remarks to each other about unwashed rent-a-mob hooligans and left-wing agitators sent by the Kremlin."

When Elaine got home, her parents were making preparations to leave, and she remembered that they were going to stay with friends in Kent for the weekend. Her mother greeted her with a list of instructions.

"Don't forget to lock up the front *and* back doors when you go to bed at night, and don't leave any windows open when you go out, and remember to unplug the iron if you use it. And *don't* stay out late, just because we're not here."

Elaine saw them off, standing in the dark street waving until the car was out of sight, then went back into the house, feeling its emptiness wrap her in a cold embrace. As her parents went out so often she was used to being alone in the house, but this was the first time they had left her to spend a whole weekend alone. She turned on the kitchen radio to break the almost tangible silence, made herself a mug of coffee, and decided to spend the evening reading a book on hunting procedures which Kate had lent her. Mark would be arriving back soon, she supposed. She wished he had suggested calling round to see her, instead of leaving it until tomorrow. Her doubts came surging back. Was she being foolish to think she meant anything to him at all? Wouldn't he have wanted to see her that evening if he had cared about her a fraction as much as she cared for him?

By the time morning came, after a night disturbed by the consciousness of being alone in the house and a heightened awareness of every gurgling pipe, she had convinced herself that Mark was totally indifferent to her. She was doubly taken aback when, arriving punctually on the doorstep, he kissed her on the cheek, told her, "You look gorgeous," and gave her a small parcel wrapped in brown paper.

"What is it?" She felt a little giddy, unable to cope with the emotional peaks and troughs he always seemed to be causing her.

"It's for you. I saw it in an antique shop."

She opened the parcel. Inside was a small Art Nouveau vase glazed in green-gold – the colour of Mark's eyes, she thought – with a raised pattern of lilies. She turned it in her hand, feeling its smooth surface.

"I thought you might like it."

"I love it. Thank you so much." The phrase sounded trite; words were inadequate to convey what she felt, after her doubts.

They got into the car and sped away, Elaine feeling that the day was off to a magical start. It was a sharply cold but bright morning, the sky flawless blue, the golds and greens and russets of the leaves brilliant in the sunshine.

"A fine scenting morning," Stuart remarked ironically, getting into the car with Kate.

The meet was to be held at a village pub some twelve miles away, but the demonstrators had arranged to gather beforehand at a nearby road junction so that their combined arrival at the meet would make more impact. Elaine looked out of the window, only half-attending to the conversation of the others. The landscape in the autumn sunlight made her wish she could paint it, capture the last wreaths of mist in the hollows, the frosting of old man's beard over the hedges, the shadows darkening the furrows of ploughed fields like the ribbing on a sweater. Her stomach was fluttering, partly with anticipation of the confrontation which lay ahead, and partly at the remembrance of the way Mark had looked at her, and the thought of spending the whole day with him.

"There's Joe's car," Kate said as they rounded a corner.

Mark pulled up behind the shabby Escort, where Joe, huddled in a green coat, was standing in a gateway with Maureen, Sue and two other women, studying a map.

"Hi, you lot," Joe called as they climbed out of the Mini. "We're just seeing where they're likely to go after the meet."

"Quite a few horseboxes and riders have gone past already," said one of the women.

"Saw last week's paper, Mark," said Maureen. "Great photographs. Well done."

"Thanks," Mark replied diffidently.

"What's the plan, then?" Stuart asked, pulling on his green waterproof coat.

"We wait till about half past ten, when most of them should be assembled," Joe explained. "Then we get out our banners and march right up to the pub."

"Have you got leaflets?" Kate asked.

Joe patted the capacious pocket of his waterproof. "Yes, and I phoned the local press yesterday, so they might be sending someone along. It would be great to get something in the paper."

"Only if they're sympathetic, though," Maureen pointed out. "Last year's report didn't do us much good."

"What happened last year?" asked one of the other women.

Maureen grimaced. "Terry, one of our more enthusiastic members, brought along a whole gang of yobbos from Northwood and it all got rather unpleasant."

Elaine remembered that it had been this time last year when Joe had been arrested. She hoped that nothing of the kind would happen today. She seemed to remember that when the occasion had first been discussed, she had volunteered for the banner demonstration only. Now she seemed to have become involved in the "sabbing" as well; Stuart and Kate and Mark were obviously planning to spend the whole day out.

The sound of an approaching vehicle made them all look up to see a pale blue Transit van drawing to a halt. The driver hooted cheerily and pulled up ahead of Joe's Escort.

"Oh, no . . ." Joe stared in disbelief as the back doors of the Transit opened, and army surplus-clad figures began to spill out. "Talk of the devil."

Maureen turned on Joe angrily. "I thought we agreed they weren't coming this time?"

"We did, but what can I do?" Joe retaliated, jutting out his beard defensively. "I don't own the countryside, do I?"

Maureen gave a heavy sigh of exasperation. "They'll ruin everything."

Tyres scrunched as a smart cream horsebox pulled carefully round the bend. The tweed-capped passenger stared curiously at the army surplus bunch. one of whom raised two fingers in a V-sign and shouted "Scum!"

"That's exactly what we don't want," Maureen said furiously.

"Well, I'll just have a word with Terry and see if I can get him to keep things calm," Joe said. "I don't see what else I can do. I can hardly tell them to go home."

Elaine looked anxiously at the khaki-clad figures as Joe walked towards them. They did look rather ominous. She wondered what they were likely to do. "Where do they all come from?" she asked Maureen.

Maureen shrugged expressively. "We don't know. Quite honestly I think they just like a bit of aggro. Which is what the rest of us try to avoid."

"Mind you, some of the hunt supporters are just as bad," Kate pointed out.

Fortunately, at that point a white Renault drew up, containing Mr and Mrs Wiseman, the grey-haired couple who had been at the meeting, and four other distinctly middle-aged passengers, which helped to restore the balance of respectability. Joe, after several minutes of earnest conversation with Terry, reported, "They're going to go straight to the wood where we think the hounds will be heading, so they won't be at the meet. They're going to spray around a bit, and look for blocked earths."

Elaine knew that hunt saboteurs carried a strongly aromatic anti-mate spray, sold in pet shops for masking the scent of bitches on heat. The aroma was powerful enough to confuse the hounds and prevent them from picking up a fox's scent. Perhaps Terry's group weren't so bad, she thought, if their efforts were likely to result in a saved fox.

"I think we'll get going," Joe said, consulting his watch.

Banners and placards were fetched from the vehicles. It was generally agreed that Kate's and Elaine's banner was the most eye-catching, so they found themselves at the front of the small procession. The others arranged themselves in pairs behind, except Mark, whose role was as photographer. Two female riders, smartly turned out in black jackets and gleaming boots and mounted on elegant thoroughbreds, drew level and passed, studiously ignoring the protestors. The sound of the hoofbeats and the sight of the sleek, powerful animals made Elaine's heart thump with excitement and nervousness.

The scene in front of them as they rounded a bend in the lane was as picturesque as a sporting print: a tiled inn with its walls decked in dark crimson Virginia creeper; horses, standing quietly or pawing the ground; scarlet-coated hunt servants; hounds, black-and-tan-and-white, with feathery tails raised in anticipation. A police car with two officers inside it waited unobtrusively in the pub's car park.

"Are they expecting trouble?" Elaine asked Kate.

"There's usually at least one car, just in case," Kate answered.

"Useful, from our point of view, as we're so greatly outnumbered," Joe added, behind them.

The procession marched determinedly forward. Their appearance had not gone unnoticed; several heads had turned in their direction and Elaine heard one of the scarlet-coated men give a loud, derisive laugh. She felt vulnerable at the head of the group, like someone walking into gunfire. As they drew nearer to the pub, several of the riders positioned their big horses in their path, so that they had to push their way through. Elaine, unused to horses, was fearful of passing so close to the big animals with their iron-shod hooves, but seeing Kate and the others marching on without a qualm she steeled herself and followed their example. "I see the loonies are here," she heard a well-bred voice remark.

They reached the public house forecourt, and positioned themselves against the wall raising their banners aloft. With more time now to survey the scene, Elaine found herself filled with conflicting emotions, part of her – she had to admit it – thrilling at the sheer spectacle: the milling hounds; the shining horses arching their necks and foaming their bits in suppressed excitement, their neat oiled hooves churning the gravel; the riders, smartly turned out in black or scarlet jackets and snowy white stocks, sitting relaxed, chatting, and sipping at drinks offered them on silver trays, while one or two had to give all their attention to controlling their excitable, wheeling horses. But another part of her was filled with anger and contempt. How could these people, obviously so concerned for the welfare of the horses they groomed and cherished, be so blind to the suffering they were about to inflict on another living creature, in the name of enjoyment?

Elaine noticed several children and teenagers on ponies among the riders: Pony Club types, some being offered advice from mothers on foot in headscarves and tweeds. Many of the riders were ignoring the protest, but Elaine was conscious of several jeers and supercilious remarks.

She noticed that one rider, a tall slim girl on a pretty dark grey horse, was staring intently in their direction. Looking back at the girl, Elaine knew that she had seen her somewhere in more familiar surroundings. Where, she couldn't think. She waggled her end of the banner to attract Kate's attention.

"Kate – that girl over there on the dark grey horse. Do we know her from somewhere?"

Kate peered through the throng of riders. "Christ. I knew I'd seen her somewhere. That's Rosalind – you know, that Caroline Radway girl."

Elaine remembered now, looking at the girl again. Her black riding coat fitted closely, flattering her slender figure, and the severe peaked cap emphasized the delicacy of her small face. She turned and said something to the rider next to her, and they both laughed.

"Has she recognized us?" Elaine said.

"Don't know. She's giving us a good once-over, anyway." Kate turned to Mark, who was fiddling with his camera. She pointed out the girl to him and said, "That's the fair Rosalind, from St. Snob's girls' school."

Mark looked at Caroline Radway with considerable interest. "Is it, indeed?" he remarked.

"It's a bit much, being expected to fraternize with blood sports supporters," Kate muttered in disgruntled tones.

"I think they're going to move off fairly soon," Joe told them. "Mark, are you going to get a photo of us? The press bod doesn't seem to have turned up."

Mark pushed his way through the horses, and Elaine saw that as he did so he passed close to Caroline, to get a better look, she supposed. Suddenly fiercely possessive, she wished Caroline wasn't quite so pretty. But she told herself that Mark was hardly likely to be interested in a member of the enemy's ranks.

By the time Mark had taken his photograph, climbing up on the bank by the hedge in order to see the banners above the crowd of horses and riders, the hounds were being gathered together with harsh reprimands and whipcracks. The foot followers stood aside, calling out "Have a good day" and "Good hunting", and the riders marshalled themselves behind the hounds and the hunt staff. The clatter of hooves on the tarmac raised a tremendous, exciting din as the horses moved off in the direction of the beech woods.

"We might as well follow them on foot till we see what direction they take," Joe said. "If we can't keep up on foot, we can go back for the cars."

"We're going back for our car n)w," said Mr Wiseman. "We'll see you later."

Several non-riding hunt supporters were preparing to follow the horses in cars and Land Rovers, and the road was blocked with vehicles and fumes.

"If we should get split up," Joe said, "we'll meet either here at the pub, or at the cars."

"We'll look out for you," said Mrs Wiseman. "Be careful you don't get *accounted for*."

Chapter Seven

Elaine, already regretting her thick sweater, was beginning to realize just how unfit she was. Feeling that she had run as much as she could, she slowed to a walk, gasping for breath. The riders were already far ahead, having set off at a fast trot. Elaine and Kate, staying together, followed the horses up a long, gradual hill and along the edge of a ploughed field, where the mud clung tenaciously to their shoes and boots. The hounds, it appeared, were now being sent into the large, dense wood which bordered two sides of the field. Mark, surprisingly fit, had run on ahead with Stuart, and was nowhere to be seen.

"We'll catch up in a minute. There's bound to be a delay while the hounds find a scent," Kate panted.

One of the hunt servants, conspicuous in his red coat and mounted on a huge, solid, grey horse, was posted at the edge of the wood, his long whip at the ready. The hounds themselves could not be seen, but the sounds of cracking twigs and shouted commands indicated that they were about their business in the shadowy depths of the wood. A line of hunt followers' cars was parked in the lane along the edge of the ploughed field, and several of the occupants were standing on the grassy bank of the verge, looking down towards the woods. Elaine and Kate, reaching the lane, hurried past, making for the point ahead of them where the wood joined the road. Elaine had no idea what they were going to do next. She wondered what was going on in the wood now. In her imagination the fox, rust-coloured like the autumn leaves, heard the hounds crashing through the undergrowth. She pictured it running in the open fields, tiring, its fur damp and bedraggled with dew and mud, its ears straining for the sounds of the keen, fit foxhounds with the scent of a kill in their nostrils. She looked at the car followers and the remaining riders strung out along the lane, not understanding how they could set out to terrify and kill a wild creature without apparently seeing anything wrong in it.

Her train of thought was interrupted by a sudden explosion of noise from the woods below, shouts and whistles and whipcracks and barking. She and Kate leaped up on the bank with the car followers. "There's one of the blighters," one of them said, angrily. Elaine guessed that he didn't mean a fox. Following his pointing finger she caught a glimpse of a khaki-clad figure running through the undergrowth, and there were angry shouts from the roadside of "Get out of there, you're trespassing!"

"All that noise should have put paid to finding a fox in this wood, at any rate," Kate muttered.

She hadn't spoken quietly enough, for a youngish man in a dark green shooting jacket and tweed cap overheard her, and directed a look of scorn at the two girls. "If you're with that lot of hooligans, you might tell your friends that they're trespassing on private land. If I had my way, I'd have the whole lot of you arrested for disrupting something that's perfectly legal."

"And if we had our way, we'd have you, and everyone else who kills animals for pleasure, chopped up and fed to your own hounds." The words were out before Elaine had time to think, surprising both herself and Kate, who shot her an impressed glance.

The man looked down his nose at her and said, "Oh, you're all the same. You don't know what you're talking about." He began to turn away, but Kate demanded, "Why do you assume that?"

The man's companion, a smaller, dumpier female version, said, "Oh, save your breath, Edward," and the man walked away without answering Kate.

Elaine knew it was a waste of time to argue with hunt supporters – they weren't likely to change their minds, to say "Oh yes, you're right, it *is* cruel, I'd never seen it like that before" – but somehow the sight of them, so cool and arrogant and resistant to change, aroused her most aggressive feelings. She began to understand how conflicts could develop, no matter how strong the pacifist leanings of people like Maureen and Joe. It was an explosive situation, each side equally intolerant of the other's point of view; a situation which could flare up at the slightest provocation, like a match set to brushwood.

"Look!" Kate pointed back down the lane, in the direction of the pub. The police car was making its way cautiously past the cars and Land Rovers which were almost blocking the narrow lane. Behind it was a white police van.

"They must have asked on their radio for reinforcements. I didn't think they'd bother," Kate said. "There are so few of us."

The police vehicles drew up in a gateway where the wood met the lane, and about ten policemen climbed out and ran into the woods, to the approval of the hunt supporters. More shouts and whistles were heard, and after a pause several of Terry's group emerged on to the road. One of them, held by a police officer, was led towards the van.

"What's happening? They can't be arrested, can they?" Elaine was concerned for Mark and Joe and Stuart, not knowing where they were.

"Not just for trespass, no. Only for assault or causing damage or something like that. Trouble is, it's often only one person's word against another's."

By the time the girls reached the wood, the hunt seemed to be leaving, put off by the commotion. The car followers were getting back into their vehicles and driving away. The police van and car left too, leaving Terry and some of his accomplices standing in the lane.

"What happened?" Kate asked urgently.

"Nothing really." Terry gave a venomous glare at the departing police van. "They just told us this was private land and we'd have to leave. But one of the redcoats said Bob threw a stone at his horse, and they've taken him in."

"He didn't, did he?" Kate asked.

"Dunno. Anyway, they're clearing off now, probably to the woods over the back. We stopped them finding anything here, by the looks of it. It reeks of anti-mate in there. See you later." Terry jogged off in pursuit of his friends.

More figures were emerging from the wood now that the police van had gone, among them Stuart, Joe and Mark, Elaine noted with relief. Mark, who had a long scratch across his nose, gave her a rueful grin.

"We didn't find any blocked earths in there, but at least we've delayed things a bit," Joe reported.

"Did you see what happened to the bloke who got arrested?" Kate asked.

"No. We were at the other end of the wood. That's why the police didn't turn us out too," Joe explained. "What's he supposed to have done?"

"Thrown a stone at a horse."

Joe raised his eyes skywards in a gesture of exasperation. "It's difficult to know what really happened, but we can do without people who'd do anything so bloody stupid."

"You don't think he really did, do you?" Elaine asked, appalled.

"Who knows? Terry's basically all right, but some of the people he brings along are a bit suspect. And of course the hunting types like to tar us all with the same brush, make out we're all like that."

"They often start it, though," Kate put in hotly. "What about that time we were spraying round some trees and two of them actually rode at us and tried to knock us over?"

"Yes, I know," Joe said placatingly. "That's why we've

got Mark here with his camera, in case anything like that happens."

"Well, I'm quite prepared to be trampled underfoot if it means Mark can get a good photograph," Kate said decisively.

They caught up with the riders, who were waiting by a larch wood further up the hill, and there was a long pause during which it seemed to Elaine that nothing at all was going on. From what she'd seen of hunting so far, she didn't think it could be very exciting for the riders. It didn't resemble sporting prints she'd seen, with horses stretched out at full gallop or leaping gates or floundering in enormous brooks. All they'd done so far was stand about.

A sudden burst of hound noise drew her attention, first one hound giving voice with an unmistakable note of excitement, then another, and another. "That's it," Joe said bitterly. "They've found." The whole pack was joining in now. Whipcracks and a long note on the horn were heard, and then the hounds were streaming away up a grassy hillside on the far side of the wood, followed by the red-coated huntsman, while the rest of the field, their horses prancing and sidling, filtered through a gateway, vanished behind the wood and reappeared higher up the hillside in joyous pursuit. Elaine, in spite of her contempt, couldn't help feeling a thrill of excitement at the dramatic surge into action, hearing the thundering of hooves carried to her on the wind, sensing the exhilaration of riding a powerful horse, controlling its strength. But you don't have to kill a fox to do that, she told herself.

"What now?" Mark was saying. "Follow on, or go back for the cars?"

"Oh, follow on." Joe was stuffing his map back into his pocket. "We'll lose them otherwise. They may check –"

Elaine ran with the others until her lungs were bursting – why did the fox have to run *uphill*, she wondered – but they couldn't compete with the horses. Even the smallest ponies had vanished by the time they reached the hilltop, only a welter of hoofprints in the mud indicating the direction they had taken. Elaine's throat rasped as she breathed in the cool air, but she was running more easily now down the edge of a ploughed field, skidding in the mud. You need to go into training for this, she thought. She was boiling hot inside her thick sweater.

They paused at the bottom of the field, listening for the horn's note, imagining it in every gust of wind. Joining a lane, they hurried along for what seemed miles; the landscape looked empty, and Elaine had lost all sense of direction.

"This is hopeless," Kate remarked. "I think we've lost them for good . . ."

"Wait!" Joe stopped dead and was pointing at a grassy field ahead of them to the right. "Look at the way those sheep are huddled together. That must mean the hunt's around."

The sheep were indeed pressed together in a compact flock, moving slowly and uneasily along the line of the hedge. A moment later the sound of the horn confirmed Joe's suggestion.

"They're coming this way! The fox may have crossed the lane . . ." At once all those with anti-mate cans had whipped them out and were spraying frantically. The hounds appeared behind the thin hedge, noses down, tails waving, following the scent. They paused on reaching the road and then turned downhill, towards the waiting group. Now the huntsman was cantering along the edge of the field, and the sound of hooves announced that the other mounted followers would soon be appearing over the brow of the field. What would happen now, Elaine wondered, picturing the massed group of riders channelled into the lane, advancing like the Charge of the Light Brigade. The air was thick with the citrus smell of anti-mate. Her instincts told her to move, climb over the wire or flatten herself against the hedge, out of the way of the oncoming tide, but the others were standing their ground.

The pack was upon them, the hounds' smooth, damp coats brushing against their legs. Reaching the invisible aromatic barrier, the hounds checked, but the huntsman had reached the road now. His face, already reddish-purple with exertion, darkened further when he saw the group ahead. He cracked his whip and urged the hounds forward, through to clear air, to find their line again. He spurred his horse on, looking straight ahead, barging between Mark and Stuart so that they were forced to leap aside.

More riders were on the road now, hunt servants first, then the ordinary followers, coming dense and fast, hooves skidding on the smooth road surface.

"Watch out!"

The protestors scattered to either side of the lane as the first riders drew level, even Kate apparently having forgotten her offer of being photographed beneath trampling hooves. One of the riders, a tall man on a large bay, deliberately wrenched his horse's head so that it plunged close to Elaine and Kate where they stood against the hedge. Grinning, he hauled at the reins, urging the horse even closer, so that Elaine, already pressed hard against the hedge, tried to force herself into it, shrinking from the large iron-shod hooves. The horse baulked, head up, eyes rolling in protest, and swerved out into the lane.

"You bastard," Stuart shouted from the opposite verge.

"If that's hunting etiquette I'm not impressed," Kate shouted furiously after the man.

"Learn some etiquette yourselves," he shouted scornfully over his shoulder.

"Are you OK?" Stuart called across to the girls, who nodded, extricating themselves from the hedge.

Most of the riders looked straight ahead as they passed. Elaine, the smells of leather and sweaty horse mingling in her nostrils, saw Caroline Radway, her face flushed and her black jacket flecked with white foam. She knew that some of the antis considered everyone who went hunting to be sadistic, consumed with blood-lust. But Kate had told her that most of the riders actually saw very little of what went on, being far behind the hounds for most of the time. It must be easy, if you were brought up with that sort of background, to go along because everyone else did it, to think it was the natural way to spend a winter Saturday, getting some healthy outdoor exercise. Caroline Radway didn't look like a sadist. How far were your opinions really your own, Elaine wondered, and how far were they conditioned by your upbringing? If she had had a tweedy Pony Club mum and a dad with a Range Rover and a shooting stick, might she have been there now on horseback, dismissing the antis as left-wing loonies?

Almost all the riders had surged past now, only a few stragglers emerging further up the lane. Elaine ran on again with the others, in the wake of the field. The riders were turning off the road, in at an open gateway, stringing out across the edge of a field planted with winter wheat, setting off at a fast canter. Two fields ahead, the leading riders had already checked; behind them the excitable horses piled up like a motorway traffic jam, snorting and wheeling.

"What's happening?" Elaine gasped.

"Don't know," Kate panted.

The check was long enough for them to catch up with the waiting riders, and to see the hounds being sent into a small dense wood. "Lost the scent, maybe," Joe muttered. "Either that, or the fox has gone to ground. We'll soon see – they'll bring on the terrier men if that's the case."

The huntsman was blowing his horn, and Elaine wondered whether this was a signal to the terrier men. Sure enough, two men in Barbour coats, with Jack Russell terriers eagerly straining at their leashes, soon appeared from the direction of the road. Kate stared at the men as they approached, then suddenly grabbed Elaine's arm.

92

"Christ, Elaine, don't let them see you. It's the men from the veal farm."

Elaine shot them a quick, surprised glance before turning her back. Kate was right. There was no mistaking the beaky features of the taller man and the short, stocky, aggressive build of the other. The men passed without a glance, looking towards the huntsman who was waiting to give them directions, and Kate let out a sigh of relief.

"Not that it matters now, but they must have connected our innocent act with the photos in the paper," she muttered to Elaine. "What bastards those men are. Not content with making money out of baby calves, they get their kicks by torturing foxes to death."

"I'm sure they won't kill the fox – not at this stage," Joe told them. "They won't want to spoil their run. It's a fairly fresh fox still – they're more likely to bolt it and carry on hunting it."

Joe proved to be right. The hounds were being made to gather beside the wood, not taken away to find a new quarry, which would have been the case if the terrier men were going to kill the fox in the earth. After a delay, the hounds gave voice in new excitement and the chase was on again, the horses glad to be off after their dull wait, the foot followers running on in pursuit across the next field. The pace was fast, but with frequent checks, so that the followers, with aching legs and searing lungs, were able to keep in touch for the first few fields. But they were slowed down by a long gradual hill, so that, reaching the top, red-faced and puffing, they could see the hunt right down in the next valley, coming out of a farm track on to a lane.

The hounds had checked on reaching the lane, and were milling about uncertainly. Further along, Terry's Transit van could be seen pulling away, revving noisily, and several figures were running across the field beyond.

"Terry's lot," Joe said. "Looks like they may have succeeded in spoiling the scent."

Huntsman and hounds seemed uncertain about what to do next, casting about in various directions. Eventually, they set off along the lane again, and Joe guessed that the huntsman had decided to try drawing a new wood.

"There's Mr and Mrs Wiseman," Kate pointed out as the white Renault appeared in the lane and drew up in a gateway.

It seemed an opportune moment to return and collect the cars, as the Wisemans were able to offer transport, albeit under rather cramped conditions. Several riders already seemed to be making their way home, and a short search found many horses clustered immobile in a gateway near a small covert, into which hounds were being sent in the hope of finding another fox. Elaine and Kate got out of Marks' Mini to see what was going on.

"It's simply miles back to the box," said a disgruntled-looking lady rider near Elaine. "I'm calling it a day. Grayling's had enough of this standing about."

"I think I'll join you," said her companion. "It gets dark so early now."

Several other riders were reaching the same decision, and were turning their horses' heads homewards. The hounds continued to search fruitlessly through the wood until the huntsman blew a long, mournful note on the horn and called the hounds together.

"That's it," Joe said triumphantly. "A successful day's sabotage."

"No foxes accounted for today – what a beastly shame," Kate said in plummy upper-class tones.

The sun was sinking as they drove home, the alders and birches purplish against its rosy light. Mark slowed to pass two horses, a bay and a grey, walking abreast.

"Caroline Radway," Kate said.

"The fair Rosalind?" Mark gave a merry toot on the horn and Caroline looked round, surprised and unrecognizing.

"Beautiful but brainless, poor thing. Or at least, we'll

94

give her the benefit of the doubt," Kate remarked, looking back along the lane, where the trees threw slanting shadows in the approaching twilight.

"Remember that day last year," Stuart reminisced, "when it poured with rain all day long, and we got lost and had to tramp miles, soaking wet, to find the car, only to discover the tyres had been let down?"

"You've had an easy introduction to sabbing," Kate told Elaine.

Rounding a corner, Mark suddenly screeched to a halt on seeing Terry's blue Transit van parked in a gateway.

"They probably don't realize the hunt's packed up," Stuart said.

They all got out of the car, to find that it was not Terry at the wheel, but a dark-haired young man with steel-rimmed glasses.

"Hi, Mike," Stuart greeted him. "Isn't Terry with you?"

"He's been arrested."

"Arrested? What the hell for?"

"Got in a slanging match with some prat in a Land Rover. Police got both of them for abusive behaviour. We're just waiting for two of our mates to turn up, then we're going to the police station to see if they're letting him out yet. Did you see the two terrier men?"

"Yes. What about them?"

"Well." Mike paused for dramatic effect. "Terry saw them just before the police took him in, and he says he's heard rumours they're involved in dog-fighting."

Chapter Eight

It seemed to Elaine that with the mere mention of dog-fighting they were entering new and more dangerous territory.

"It's a matter for the police," Stuart said firmly.

"I think you're right," Kate agreed. "But what actual evidence is there to go on?"

"Not enough," said Mark. "Just because the chap's got a bull terrier, the police aren't going to read anything into that. There must be thousands of bull terriers in the country. It's not illegal to keep them."

"It all seems to fit in, though," Elaine said. "The muzzle in the kennel at the farm, and the men coming in with the dog in a van, and not liking us going near the kennels."

They were in Kate's kitchen, drinking tea while Kate and Stuart prepared beans on toast. Elaine, lifting the fat black-and-white cat on to her knee, assimilated the new information. Dog-fighting, unlike fox-hunting, was illegal, and carried heavy fines. She knew from newspapers, and articles by the RSPCA and the League Against Cruel Sports, that it was carried out in strictest secrecy.

"Does Terry think they actually hold the fights on the farm?" Kate asked.

"It seems likely, doesn't it?" said Stuart, tipping beans into a saucepan. "It's very remote, with no houses within earshot, and they've got that huge barn."

"Surely, all we'd need to do would be to get the police to go and look at the barn, and see if there's any evidence of dog-fighting taking place?" Elaine suggested. "They don't actually have to catch them red-handed, do they?"

"No," Kate agreed, turning over the toast. "There was

that case recently of dog-fighting arranged by the caretaker of a junior school. The police just found bloodstains and equipment and so on."

"They found a dead dog," Mark reminded her. "And they must have had a better tip-off than we can give them. All we can say, basically, is that the chap's got a bull terrier and we don't like his face."

"I suppose we do need a bit more to go on – " Stuart began, looking doubtful.

Mark cut in impatiently. "There's one excellent reason why we should do something ourselves rather than call in the police."

Stuart turned round from the saucepan of beans he was stirring and gave Mark a disbelieving stare. "Do something ourselves? You've got to be kidding, Mark."

"It's too serious," Elaine agreed.

"If you're thinking of bursting in on a dog-fight, or something heroic like that, you can just forget it," Stuart continued. "You don't realize how tough these guys are. They won't think twice about beating us up, girls included."

Mark glared back at him. "Well, this is a golden opportunity for us, if you could just see it. It's not just anybody involved in dog-fighting, is it? It's the *hunt terrier men*. If we could get just one photograph . . ."

There was a silence while the impact of Mark's words was felt. All of them knew how anxious the field sports organizations were to deny any association with the illegal sports – dog-fighting, cock-fighting and badger-baiting – which they admitted were disgustingly cruel. Any proof of a link with the disreputable and illegal sport of dog-fighting, if publicized, would weaken the case of all the legitimate field sports in the public eye.

"Well, what about it?" Mark prompted. "If we could get just one photograph, we could sell it to the popular daily papers, along with a photo of the terrier men out with the

97

hunt. As for the danger – well, there's safety in numbers. If we take enough people we should come off best, even if there was a fight. The girls don't have to come if they don't want to."

Kate glared at him belligerently. "If there's anything going on, you can count us in on it."

"I suppose Mark's got a point," Elaine said. "If he did get a photograph then we'd have something concrete to show the police, as well."

"Well . . ." Stuart was weakening. "Suppose we don't decide anything until tomorrow. We've still got to find out, somehow, when and what time it takes place, remember."

Much later, Mark drove Elaine home. She could sense his excitement at the prospect of exposing the dog-fight. It was a new challenge for him, just as entering the veal farm had been. She felt that her own mood was quite at odds with his, the temporary elation at having saved a fox completely submerged by the realization that cruelty to animals was a bottomless pit. The triumph over the saved fox seemed childish to her now. What was one fox, on one day of the hunting season, when countless thousands of animals suffered daily in laboratories and factory farms and slaughterhouses? And now the dog-fighting, perhaps the worst cruelty of all, because people went along, not for a ride or a day out in the country, but for the sole purpose of seeing animals injure or kill each other. For Mark, she knew, it was an opportunity to get the better of the terrier men, to expose the link with hunting. He was looking forward to it almost with enjoyment, not wasting time in futile sorrow for the fate of animals which couldn't be saved anyway.

"You're quiet," Mark said, interrupting her thoughts. She looked up, realizing that they were already in her own road, and that she'd hardly spoken to him throughout the drive home.

"Oh, sorry. Just thinking about the dog-fighting and

everything – how much cruelty there is, and how little we can do to stop it."

"No point worrying about it." Mark pulled up outside the dark house. "Just think about the things you *can* do something about."

"Mm. I suppose you're right." She looked at the blank windows of the unwelcoming house. The thought of its emptiness was not inviting. "Would you like to come in for a bit?" she asked Mark on an impulse. She saw him hesitate, and added "My parents have gone away for the weekend."

"Have they?" Mark looked considerably more interested. "OK, then. I'm in no hurry to get back."

She led the way into the lounge, where she drew the curtains and switched on the lamps to give a more congenial atmosphere. She searched through her parents' music collection to find something Mark would like, choosing a Mozart piano concerto.

"It's very smart, isn't it?" Mark hadn't taken the chair she offered, but was standing up looking around the room, at the expensive pottery on the back-lit wall unit, the screenprint above the fireplace, and the few glossy books on the shelves.

"Yes. It's my parents' taste, not mine," Elaine said, feeling for some reason that she needed to apologize.

"What would you have, then?"

"I don't know. Something more lived-in, less formal. I like Kate's house, where everything's more shabby than this, but you feel you can relax." Mark sat down on the sofa as she spoke, looking perfectly relaxed, not tensed up and on edge as she felt herself. It was ridiculous, she told herself. He hadn't come to judge her. "I'd like lots of plants, and cats – my parents won't have one because of hairs on the furniture – and original paintings instead of reproductions," she finished.

"Mm. That's not a bad screenprint, though." Mark

99

narrowed his eyes and looked at it critically. "Which reminds me. You've never shown me any of your drawings and paintings."

"I've never seen any of yours, either," she pointed out, "apart from the scenery for the play."

"I didn't know you wanted to see them. I've got loads at the flat. I'll show them to you next time you come round."

"Thank you. I'd love to see them."

"But only if you show me yours now." He smiled at her lazily, lounging on the sofa.

"Oh – " She hesitated, thinking of her scruffy folder of watercolours and pencil drawings, none of them framed. She was sure they wouldn't be able to compete with his undoubtedly superior efforts. "Well, I will, but you won't think much of them, I warn you."

She fetched the folder from her bedroom and watched him leaf through the contents. He was going to judge her, after all. He examined each one closely, without comment, his profile stern and noncommittal. She looked at his dark eyelashes, his staight, aristocratic nose with the bramble scratch across it, his broad, intelligent forehead, his smooth tanned skin with dark stubble just beginning to show through at his chin and upper lip; she remembered the clean, masculine smell of him when he had kissed her. He looked well-groomed even after a day spent running round the countryside. She couldn't believe that someone so desirable was still interested in her. Perhaps he wouldn't be, now that he knew how childish her artistic fumblings were. His silence was ominous, she felt. Perhaps he thought the pictures were so appalling that he couldn't think of anything tactful to say about them.

At last he finished his scrutiny, and turned to face her while she awaited his verdict. He paused, weighing his words carefully before he spoke. "You've obviously got talent," he told her. "Some of these are really promising."

Elaine could sense that a "But – " was hanging in the air,

like a school report which started, "Elaine has worked consistently, but—"

Mark leafed through the sheets and turned up one of her least favourites, a life drawing done at school for exam practice. It was a picture of a sixth form volunteer sitting on a hard-backed chair, dressed in tennis clothes. The time limit had been tight, Elaine remembered; she'd been forced to rush, and it showed in the finished drawing, with much bolder strokes and shading than she usually used. "This one, for example," Mark said. "A really convincing pose and a bold treatment."

"Oh." Elaine felt nonplussed. "What about this one?" She handed him a pencil drawing of the school gardener, a portrait which she privately felt was her best effort to date.

Mark scrutinized the drawing again before replying. "It's good, undoubtedly, but it lacks the vigour of the other one. The drawing's very accurate, but it's a bit wooden."

Elaine felt hurt, as stung as if it were meant as a personal criticism. She told herself impatiently not to be so silly; she had known he wasn't likely to go into raptures, after all. Mark was continuing, "As for the paintings, they're very competent, but I wonder if you're limiting yourself by sticking to watercolours. Some of these would be better done in oils, I think. You could widen your range, then. But these landscapes are certainly promising. They're very expressive."

"Expressive" was, Elaine thought, Mark's highest term of praise, and she felt slightly mollified.

"Perhaps the art lessons at school are a bit limiting, as well," Mark added. "Rules for exam success, and all that rot. You'd probably find it helpful to go to classes at the Adult Education Centre, where they're not quite so hidebound. You'd meet other people, and see different ways of working."

Elaine swept up the scattered sheets, wanting to put them out of sight as quickly as possible. She hadn't wanted

101

to show them to Mark and now she felt that she could only see them as he did – the dull work of a pupil taught by an old man in a backwater, out of touch with the real world of art and artists in which Mark seemed so at home.

He touched her arm. "Hey, I haven't upset you, have I? I only wanted to be helpful. I *do* think you've got talent, and you should certainly persevere."

"Well, thanks." She told herself that all he said was true, and that if she did want to improv' she must accept critisism. She knew that when she looked at his paintings it wouldn't be on the same footing at all. She would be the pupil looking at the master's work; criticism would be out of place. "Would you like some coffee now?" she asked, rising to her feet."

"Thanks."

She prepared the coffee and carried it in on a tray. The Mozart record had finished, and Mark had replaced it with something else vaguely familiar, a violin concerto in which the melody rose like a great sob, joyous and melancholy at the same time, appropriate enough for Elaine's muddled feelings. She handed Mark his coffee and sat down in the armchair next to the stereo.

"Why don't you come and sit here?" He patted the sofa next to him, looking at her with eyes dark and serious in the subdued light.

She hesitated, then moved across, and he swung his arm casually around her shoulders as she sat down. "We must make arrangements for getting on with the scenery," he told her. "There isn't long. You could come round tomorrow, if you like, and we could do some before we meet Kate and Stuart."

"That's a good idea. I haven't planned to do anything else."

They finished their coffee, but Mark made no move to go. He began to kiss her, very gently, his fingers stroking her jaw and her neck. The closeness of him was so overwhelming that she could think of nothing else, letting herself sink into the warmth of his embrace, her face against the roughness of his sweater. He pulled her closer and kissed her forehead. "Oh, Elaine," he murmured, his lips brushing her hair. "You're so lovely."

"So are you," she murmured back, touched. "I love being with you."

"Mmmm." His arms were holding her close, his lips tickling her ear. She felt heady, as if she'd been drinking wine, from the combined effects of the evocative violin music and the closeness of Mark after the day's tension. Yet at the same time, as if detached from herself, she felt a stirring of doubt. Mark was as good at this as he was at everything else, and she didn't delude herself that his accomplished performance didn't result from experience. He was considerably older than she, undoubtedly more experienced in terms of relationships – how many girls had he kissed as he was kissing her now? And for how long was he going to be satisfied with just that? Even while the thought was framing itself in her mind, his kisses were becoming more insistent, his hands no longer just holding her but gradually making exploratory moves, one hand on her thigh, the other finding its way inside her jumper . . . She pulled herself away.

"What's the matter?" His eyes, dreamy and innocent, focused on her face.

"Nothing . . . I . . ." She floundered and stopped, not wanting to appear suspicious, not knowing what to say.

"Oh, come here. I'll behave myself, I promise." He grinned at her wickedly, his white teeth gleaming in the lamplight. He clasped her gently, making her lean against him, and for a while they sat almost motionless, the music washing over them. Mark's hand stroked Elaine's hair, making her feel like a soothed child. Her emotions were as confused as ever. He seemed to have a peculiar knack of arousing conflict in her, she thought. Nothing was ever

103

stable or ordinary, as other people's relationships seemed to be, but perhaps that was what attracted her to him. Her glance strayed towards the clock. She had lost all sense of time, and now saw that it was quite late. She wondered how soon Mark would get up to go, and the realization came to her that he wouldn't, not until she told him to. Why had she been so unsuspecting as to tell him her parents had gone away? How naïve can you get, she asked herself angrily. He had probably taken her casual remark as an invitation; he was used to sophisticated girls like Zoë in the art gallery, not bumbling idiots like herself. Now she had got herself into a situation she wasn't sure how to handle. She couldn't just stand up and brightly say, "Isn't it time you went home?" And yet, even while she was thinking this out, it was so nice to be sitting close to him, feeling the warmth of his body through his sweater and his breath soft against her cheek. She didn't want to bring it to an abrupt end, sending him away into the night and going up to the cold silence of her room.

The record finished and Mark got up to turn it over. Now would be the time to suggest that it was rather late, she knew, but she said nothing, and Mark sat down beside her again, shuffling into a more comfortable position so that they were both half-lying. He put a hand under her chin and turned her head so that he could look into her face, so closely that she could see her own reflection in his dark eyes, the tenderness in his face making her limbs melt. Surely she had been misjudging him, thinking him merely calculating? He appeared to be as genuinely moved as she was by the music and the moment. He kissed her again, and even while she responded, her arm twining around his neck, she was aware of new doubts, this time concerning her own conduct. Couldn't she be accused of deliberately leading him on, inviting him in and telling him her parents were away? She knew that there were several unpleasant names for girls who encouraged boys in such a way, only to back off at the last minute.

"What's the matter?" Mark felt her sudden tension and looked up at her, quizzical and affectionate.

"I was just thinking . . ." she faltered. "Perhaps you ought to go home now."

His eyebrows shot up. "Go home now? What on earth for? You like being here with me, don't you?"

"You know I do," she whispered, her arguments fading as his fingers stroked her cheek and he pulled her down to him again.

"Just relax, then."

It was impossible to counteract his air of having everything under control, of knowing exactly what he was doing. As always she was following his lead, waiting for him to take the initiative. Soon he was kissing her passionately, kissing her neck, her eyes, her ears, while one hand crept underneath her sweater and began to undo the buttons of her shirt. He had levered himself up on one elbow so that he was almost lying on top of her, his weight crushing her. She began to struggle. "Mark, stop it!" She tried to wriggle into an upright position. "Please . . ."

He sat up too, his hair tousled for once, and looked at her in exasperation. "Now what?"

"I didn't mean this to happen." She pushed her tangled hair from her face.

"It doesn't look as if anything is going to happen, does it?"

"I really think you should go," she told him seriously.

"Do you really?" He spoke more gently, clasping her hand in his warm grip. For a moment he looked so downcast that she impulsively put her arms round him, pressing her face against his shoulder.

He kissed her hair and whispered, "I don't really have to go at all, you know."

"Oh, Mark." She was glad that her face was hidden against her sweater. "You must."

"But why?" He pushed her upright, forcing her to look at him. "You do love me, don't you?"

105

"Yes," she whispered.

She hoped he would tell her that he loved her too, but he continued, "Well, why push me out in the cold, then?" He was stroking her neck, sending intoxicating shivers down her spine, lulling her towards acceptance. "It would be so lovely . . . You needn't worry, I'll take care of every-thing."

His subtle reference to the practical considerations jolted her, a cold touch of realism at odds with the romantic atmosphere. Afterwards, when at her insistence he had finally gone, she wondered whether she had understood correctly. Did he mean that he just happened to have a contraceptive in his pocket, just in case? Had he planned everything, counting on her willingness? But then he couldn't have done – he hadn't known her parents would be away. She could only suppose that he was so confident of his romantic prowess that he was always prepared for a chance encounter.

She spent a second anxious night, lying in her solitary bed and thinking that she could have had Mark there with her. On the one hand, it seemed infinitely desirable, the very thought sending shivers down her body. But on the other hand, she felt herself instinctively backing off, not ready for such a commitment. It was only that morning – though it seemed an age ago – that she had lain there telling herself that he was totally indifferent to her. Now, in spite of the day's events, she felt little the wiser. He had a maddening way of never letting her feel sure about him, never letting her know his feelings, always leaving her doubting. Was it deliberate, she wondered, so that she was always left agonizing, grateful for his every attention?

She reached out to touch the little bronze Art Nouveau vase on her bedside table, remembering how over-whelmingly happy she'd been when he gave it to her. Now her own bungling had spoiled all that. Some of the girls at school, who talked about sex so flippantly, as if it were taken for granted that everyone treated it as casually as they appeared to, would laugh at her if they knew how naïvely she'd behaved. Several of them would, she knew, have taken up Mark's offer without hesitation, not worrying about the consequences, and told their friends all about it afterwards. It was not the sort of thing Elaine would discuss with anyone.

Next morning she wondered whether Mark would still want her to go to his flat to work on the scenery. He hadn't seemed exactly annoyed when he'd left last night, but he had certainly withdrawn from her a little, whether offended or disappointed or just plain exasperated – she couldn't tell. Armed with her drawing equipment and paintbrushes, she rang his doorbell about an hour and a half before they were due to meet Kate and Stuart.

It was Robin who answered the door, and she felt, on the whole, relieved that he was in. Mark was upstairs reading the Sunday newspapers, and he looked up when she walked in, as if surprised to see her.

"I'm sorry about last night," she whispered as soon as Robin left the room.

He shrugged, not looking at her. "Doesn't matter. Do you want a cup of tea?"

"Yes, please." She looked blankly at the *Sunday Times* colour supplement while he boiled the kettle. This was awful. He wasn't in the slightest bit pleased to see her. Why did I come, she thought.

Things improved somewhat when Robin came in and drank tea with them, making conversation easier, and then Mark brought out the scenery designs, which they discussed and worked on until it was time to leave. It's business as usual, Elaine thought as they walked to Kate's house. But only business. He made no move to put things back on a more personal level, and she felt too constricted to take such an initiative herself.

Chapter Nine

Mr Parsonage seemed irritable and abstracted, his mind not really on *Sons and Lovers*. After a half-hearted discussion, he set the class to work on an essay plan while he sat gnawing his thumbnail and frowning at some notes.

When the bell rang for the end of the lesson, he reminded them to be prompt for the first rehearsal of *As You Like It*. "God knows how we're ever going to put this play on," he added despairingly. "David Easton's got glandular fever – we've got no Orlando."

"That's a difficult one," Kate remarked as she and Elaine paused outside the Computer Room before going to their separate lessons. "He's already scraped the barrel right down to the wood, roping in people like Darren Griffiths. There's no one left to play Orlando. Unless he does it himself."

"Or gets a girl to do it," Elaine said. "That would really be confusing. A girl who the audience is supposed to think is a boy, chatting up another girl who's also pretending to be a boy, but who the audience knows is really supposed to be a girl . . ."

"Even Shakespeare would be baffled," Kate agreed. "See you at lunch time."

Later, in a quiet corner of the common room, they discussed the arrangements which had been proposed for exposing the dog-fight. After much arguing, it had been agreed to co-opt Terry and some of his friends for this particular venture, for the safety of added numbers. Clearly, four people, of whom two were girls, were not going to be a match for a group of burly men, should physical force become necessary. "Which we sincerely hope it won't," Stuart commented. The idea was for Mark to conceal himself and take a photograph from which one or both of the terrier men could be identified; the others were going simply as back-up. The main problem for the moment was to find out when the fights took place. Stuart had said that he thought they would, most likely, take place during daylight hours: "There's no need for artificial lighting then, which might attract attention, and besides, sounds carry more at night." The plan was, for the time being, to carry out surreptitious daily visits to the farm, but the practical difficulties of this were only too apparent, with all the conspirators either working or at school.

"I've been thinking about that," Elaine told Kate. "It seems to me we've overlooked something blindingly obvious."

"Oh?"

"I don't think they hold the dog-fights at the farm at all."

"What?" Kate frowned, straining to hear above the din of heavy rock music which blasted forth at that moment from a cassette player in the corner.

"Turn it down!" several people yelled, and Elaine repeated what she had said. "We've forgotten that the public footpath runs right past the barn. They're hardly likely to hold a dog-fight within a few feet of anyone who happens to stroll through, are they?"

"Christ, how stupid we are," Kate agreed. "Why on earth didn't we think of that before?"

"And the other thing I thought of is that both times you've been up there – the Sunday we did the photos and the Sunday before that, when you just went to look – there's been someone taking dogs away or bringing them back."

"Hey, you two, have you heard about David Easton?" Danny Webster flopped down in an armchair beside them. "We're Orlando-less."

"Yes, we know," Kate told him. "But actually, if you

wouldn't mind, we're trying to have an important private discussion."

"Fair enough," Danny said amiably. "Girl talk, I suppose, not for male ears. How to mend ladders in tights and stop your eyeshadow from smudging." He ducked to avoid a flying book hurled by Kate. "OK, OK, I know when I'm not wanted."

"Good," said Kate, turning to Elaine. "Now, what were you saying?"

"What I think is that perhaps they have the fights on Sunday, but go somewhere else to do it, somewhere more remote."

"It makes sense, doesn't it?" Kate said thoughtfully. "And if you're right, it would make tracking them down so much easier, knowing it's likely to be on a Sunday, I mean. We'd just have to lurk about and follow them wherever they go."

"Without letting them see us. Remember what Stuart said – how secretive they'd be, with lookouts and everything. It won't be that easy. We can't go charging after them in a great big Transit van," Elaine pointed out.

"No." Kate frowned meditatively, chewing the end of a pencil. "We'll have to think it out very carefully. Is Mark at school today?"

"He'll be here for the rehearsal this afternoon."

There was no opportunity to speak to Mark before the rehearsal, and when they entered the theatre he was in earnest conversation with Mr Parsonage, who was looking decidedly more cheerful. The grammar school girls and their hatchet-faced teacher had arrived punctually, and were all clutching their brand new copies of *As You Like It*, ready to start.

"We've had to make a few changes in the casting," Mr Parsonage said when everyone had stopped chatting. "David Easton, who was to play Orlando, is ill with glandular fever. Luckily, Mark here has kindly agreed to

110

take over Orlando, and Susan will play Jacques. This'll mean some doubling-up with the minor parts . . .'

He went on to explain. Elaine and Kate exchanged amazed glances. "He *what*?" Kate hissed in Elaine's ear. "Agreed to play Orlando with that blood sports supporter as Rosalind? How on earth did he get talked into that one?"

Elaine, watching Mark, who was looking across the theatre at Caroline Radway, wondered how much persuasion had been necessary. Why is Mark the only person who can do anything, she thought viciously. He wasn't even a proper pupil of the school. He enjoyed the attention, she knew, whether it was acting or scene-painting or taking photographs for Animal Rights; perhaps it was all the same to him. Caroline Radway was looking particularly attractive today, in a long white diamond-patterned sweater and black jeans, with a brilliant turquoise scarf knotted around her slender neck. She smiled across at Mark, looking decidedly pleased by the change of cast. Or, Elaine wondered, was it just her own imagination? Was she being unnecessarily jealous and possessive over Mark?

Mr Parsonage approached Elaine as they all began to split up into their separate groups. He gave her an unctuous grin, which meant he was going to ask her to do something. "As I was just explaining, Mark's got this much larger part to learn now, so I'm taking him off scenery. He tells me that the designs are all completed, so it's just a matter of getting the work done. He said you and Sita would be able to manage it between you."

Elaine stared at Mr Parsonage until, thinking she hadn't heard him, he was about to say it all over again. She managed to cover her indignation with a polite smile. "Oh, I don't mind doing the spade work, now that the real creative effort's been put in," she said bitterly, and stalked off to join Miss Blackburn for Act 1 Scene 1. As she strode across the theatre she almost bumped into Alistair, who

111

gave her an aloof smile. She had heard earlier that day that he was going out with Sita now, and had tried to feel pleased by the news. Both he and Sita were so nice that they would suit each other, she felt, and yet she was conscious of a faint, undefined resentment. Why, she didn't know. She told herself off for wanting it all ways: preferring Mark, but still expecting Alistair to remain loyal to her.

She joined Miss Blackburn's group, feeling decidedly prickly. In her role as Adam, the manservant, she was in the opening scene with Mark as Orlando and Danny Webster as Oliver. Mark gave her a slightly apologetic smile of greeting.

"This production would come to a grinding halt without you, Mark," she returned. "How does it feel to be indispensable?" She had meant to sound flippant, and was surprised by the sarcasm in her voice.

"Oh, I'm used to it," Mark replied promptly, with one of his half-grins, so that she didn't know whether to take him seriously or not.

They read through as far as the middle of Scene 2, where a fight was to take place between Orlando and a huge wrestler played by a hulking boy who had had to specially co-opted from the fifth year, as none of the sixth form boys were outstandingly large. They were joined by Mr Parsonage and his group, which included Caroline, and Kate in her role of Touchstone. It was during this scene that the "love-at-first-sight" meeting between Orlando and Rosalind was to take place, and Elaine felt uncomfortable stirrings of jealousy at the intimacies which were to take place between Mark and Caroline. Curse David Easton for getting glandular fever, she thought gloomily.

"We won't do the wrestling bit now, obviously," Miss Blackburn said briskly. "Just carry straight on."

"Are they going to strip to the waist?" Elaine heard Caroline murmur to Sophie, the girl who was playing Celia.

"I hope so," Sophie murmured back. Caroline's hazel

eyes were fixed on Mark, and as he turned and caught her gaze she looked away with a practised flutter of her eyelashes. Elaine, watching, wished she didn't feel such a pang at witnessing this exchange. You always knew you weren't the only one who found him attractive, she told herself. She wished she could feel Kate's evident assurance that Mark would want nothing to do with a blood sports supporter. Might things have been different if she had let Mark stay on Saturday night? Was he hurt and offended, trying to show that he didn't care? Or had he simply chalked her up as a failure, to be put behind him?

She had no more to say in Scene 2, and afterwards wondered why she had stayed there. She needn't have heard the fervour with which Caroline pronounced "O excellent young man!", nor seen Mark, at the end of the scene, accompanying his words "But heavenly Rosalind!" with a direct and lingering glance at Caroline. It seemed to Elaine that there were undertones on both sides which had nothing to do with the play.

She was sure that Kate, whose matter-of-fact exterior concealed a rare perception, had noticed it, too. At the end of the rehearsal, when people were standing about chatting, Elaine hastily averted her eyes from the sight of Mark moving over to talk to Caroline. "Come on, we'll tell him what you think about the dog-fighting," Kate told her. "Don't let him see that you mind," she added in a low voice.

Thankful for her friend's moral support, Elaine made her way towards Mark as he parted from Caroline. She outlined her idea briefly, in businesslike tones, and was gratified that Mark listened seriously. He agreed that they would have to find some way of following the men undetected. "If only we had CB radios, we could arrange to swap cars so that they don't get suspicious," he suggested.

"Now that *is* an idea," Kate said approvingly. "Terry might be able to help out there. They use them for sabbing, sometimes. I'll get in touch with him tonight."

113

"What's happened about the abusive behaviour?" Mark asked.

"He'll have to appear in court, but he doesn't know when," Kate told him.

"See you tomorrow at the rehearsal," Elaine said, turning to leave.

"Hey, wait a minute." Mark caught her arm. "Are you doing anything now, or just going home?"

"Just going home, I suppose. I don't know what I'll be doing later," she added airily, remembering Kate's advice.

Still holding her arm, he moved closer to her, and said quietly, "Don't rush off. Let's go somewhere together. I've got the car outside."

He was looking at her in such a way that the words "Wouldn't you rather take Caroline?" withered on her lips. "OK, then," she replied. She managed to stop herself from sounding too eager, and saw Kate's expression, a mixture of resignation and amusement, as she tactfully melted away.

Elaine hoped that Caroline and Sophie were watching as she got into Mark's car with him. As they sped away from school, scattering dried leaves and lower-school pupils, he grasped her hand and smiled at her briefly, and she knew she was lost again, all the familiar longing for him returning with stomach-thumping intensity. It was no good telling herself he was conceited, attention-seeking, a flirt – it made no difference whatsoever.

The grey, overcast afternoon, with dusk swiftly approaching, could do little to dampen her spirits. Mark drove through the town and out to the common, where women in headscarves were walking dogs. He drew up in front of the Grove Hotel, a stately building with a sweeping front drive, and led the way through the reception area and into the lounge, where tea was being served. To Elaine, more accustomed to the coffee bar in the High Street with its jukebox and formica-topped tables, it looked like something out of *Country Life* magazine, with its soft lighting, comfortable sofas in William Morris prints, bowls of late roses, and huge brick fireplace with a tapestry screen. The only other occupants were a group of elderly ladies in tweed suits and wool dresses, and Elaine looked down at her own attire – green cord jeans and a Vegetarian Society sweatshirt – feeling that cashmere and pearls would have been more appropriate. It was typical of Mark to choose somewhere stylish and out-of-the-ordinary. He looked perfectly at home, neatly dressed as always, and ordering the tea as if he came here every day. The waitress was young and blonde and pretty, and even in the brief exchange of ordering tea Elaine could see that Mark had charmed her with the complimentary directness of his gaze, just as he seemed capable of charming every female under the age of fifty, with an enviable ease and nonchalance. But now Elaine didn't mind; it was flattering, after all, that he could attract anyone he chose, but he had chosen her.

They were both in a light-hearted mood, devouring all the cakes and scones which were placed in front of them, making silly remarks about the play, and laughing at anything. The elderly ladies smiled at them tolerantly, because, Elaine supposed, they presented a picture of carefree young love. Mark paid the bill and they drifted out, pausing in the foyer for him to direct a torrent of abuse at a dung-coloured oil painting which occupied a prominent position.

"You still haven't shown me *your* paintings," Elaine reminded him.

"No? Well, there's no time like the present, if you've got time to come round to the flat."

The contrast between this and her last visit, when Mark had been so off-hand, struck Elaine as they climbed the stairs. Robin was in, paint-spattered and reeking of turpentine, and apparently glad of an excuse to break off from his work. He talked to Elaine while Mark rummaged in cupboards and under beds, and leaned the paintings against the banisters on the landing.

Elaine looked at them. At a glance she could see that any criticism would be quite beyond her; Mark's technical skill was undeniable. There was a range of styles: abstracts in singing colours; harsh caricatures in black-and-white; expressionist oil paintings with frenzied lines, reminding her of Munch or Van Gogh; delicate Pre-Raphaelite fantasies, like the drawing he had done of her. There was no particular style which could be identified as Mark's own; the paintings were impersonal, giving away nothing. She thought of the way she felt when people looked at her own work – vulnerable, exposed, as if she was offering part of herself for approval or rejection. Mark's were like a screen behind which he kept himself concealed.

The feeling disturbed her, cancelling out her former high spirits, and making her wonder how well she knew Mark, after all. The paintings were accomplished, but there was something hollow about them. She remembered watching a piano competition on television with Alistair once, and not understanding how the judges could possibly choose a winner; the competitors all seemed to her fantastically gifted, with fingers rippling up and down the keyboard without hesitation over all the pitfalls of wrong notes. "It's something beyond technical skill they're looking for," Alistair had tried to explain. "They expect everyone to reach a high technical standard, but to win it you have to have something else – a feeling for the music – you have to be a *musician*."

Elaine thought of this, looking at Mark's paintings. It was clear that, metaphorically speaking, he could play all the right notes, but whether there was anything beyond that, she felt less sure.

Chapter Ten

By the time Sunday came, damp and grey and cheerless, Elaine was beginning to have severe misgivings about the dog-fighting. It seemed so fraught with dangers, and so unlikely that they would succeed, that the alternative of calling the police seemed temptingly straightforward. But, she reminded herself, they would need to have firm evidence that a dog-fight was taking place, so they would have to proceed with Plan A (waiting at the farm to see what happened) even if not with Plan B (trying to take photographs). Glancing out of the window at the steady drizzle, she shivered and took an extra sweater out of her wardrobe.

Downstairs, her mother, who was expecting friends for lunch, was putting a joint of lamb into the oven. "What are you doing today, Elaine?" she asked as her daughter entered the kitchen.

Elaine looked at the joint with distaste. "Seeing Kate and some other friends. We're all going round to Mark's," she replied, with perfect truth.

"Done all your school work?" asked her father, polishing wine glasses with a tea towel.

"Yes. I did it all last night." Elaine thought of her boring Saturday evening, writing notes about Lenin and Trotsky and trying to learn Adam's lines for Act 1 Scene 3. She'd expected to see Mark, but he'd phoned to say that some old friends from art college had unexpectedly called in and wanted him to go out for a meal with them. Elaine had tried not to feel resentful that he hadn't asked her to join them – they would be talking about old times and people she didn't know, she supposed.

"I hope your lunch party goes well," she told her parents as she left, pausing in the hall to collect her waterproof coat, wellingtons, scarf and spare sweater.

Outside Mark's flat, she noticed Stuart's car and a black Mini van with anti-vivisection stickers plastered over the windscreen.

"Did you have a good time last night, with your friends?" she asked Mark when he opened the door.

"Oh – yes, thanks." He gave her a perfunctory kiss, and led the way upstairs.

Kate, Stuart and Robin were in the sitting room, with Terry's friends, Sandra, who wore jet black eye make-up to match her black hair, and Mike and Pete, who had been at the opening meet.

"Terry and Dave have already gone up to the farm, just in case anything happens early," Mark told Elaine. "The rest of us are going to wait here for a bit. There's no point in a whole gang of us hanging around so early in the day."

"Especially as it's quite possible nothing at all will happen," Stuart added.

Mark produced coffee and Sunday papers, and they all settled down to wait. There were nine people, Elaine counted, taking into account the absent Terry and Dave; then she altered her total to ten on realizing that Robin was including himself in their number. Ten was quite reasonable, she thought, if there was any trouble. Even though three of them were girls, several of the boys were reasonably formidable in terms of size and strength.

The time dragged past. It was like waiting at the dentist's for an appointment that never came, Elaine thought. She hardly knew which would be worse – the anti-climax of nothing happening at all, or the sickening reality of coming face to face with a dog-fight and the sadists who initiated it.

At last Stuart said he thought it was time for them all to go up to the farm. He outlined the plans: "The men have only got three choices of direction when they leave the farm – back towards the town, on towards Alders End, or right towards Buntingfield. We'll take three cars – mine, Mark's and Pete's – and park them a mile or so from the farm, one in each direction. Then, with the CBs which Terry's rigged up for us, we can let each other know which way they've gone."

"How are you going to stop them from realizing they're being followed?" Mike asked doubtfully.

"All that we could think of," Stuart said, "was to try to swap the cars around if we can. It's the best we can do, apart from obviously dropping back as far as possible behind them. We've all got OS maps, so if we do get separated we can easily meet up again."

"Who's going into the farm this time?" Elaine asked.

"How about Kate, you, and Mike? You two girls know the layout. Go in round the back of the veal unit, not through the yard. Mike's got the CB, so you can let us know what's going on."

"And what will happen to us when you lot go roaring off in cars?" Kate asked. "You're not expecting us to run along behind?"

"Not unless you feel like the exercise," Stuart said. "We'll get one of the cars to stop for you. It might be a bit of a squash, but we'll manage. So, if you see the men leave in their vans, go and wait in the road as soon as you've told us which way they've gone. Ready, then? Got your camera gear, Mark?"

"Don't forget to take the stickers off your windscreen," Kate reminded Pete as they clattered downstairs.

Creeping through the sopping wet brambles and stinging nettles behind the veal unit, her damp jeans already clinging coldly to her legs, Elaine was struck by the faintly ludicrous nature of it all – a group of otherwise fairly sane people, spending their Sunday afternoon playing at commandos, creeping about in the wet with their

CB radios, and knowing full well that the whole operation might be totally futile. The terrier men might be sitting indoors watching television, for all they knew. The thought of the veal calves standing in their stalls just the other side of the barn's heavy timber wall served as a reminder of the pitifully small distance any of their actions could really take towards the reduction of animal suffering. For all the elation they had felt at getting Mark's photographs in the local paper, what had it really accomplished? Ruffled a few consciences, perhaps, in people who would more than likely have forgotten all about the photographs by the time they were next offered veal. The familiar wave of helplessness swept over her. It was just like the opening meet, when dozens of people had been running round the countryside to save one fox. It was all on such a small scale, such a hopeless expenditure of man-hours for such an insignificant result. But what else could you do? The only alternative seemed to be to stay at home and do nothing. She reminded herself that, after all, dog-fighting was on a different level of importance. It was against the law; details of convictions were reported in the national newspapers. Perhaps this time they really did stand a chance of achieving something, although the prospect seemed increasingly unlikely as they waited, numbed by cold and damp.

Terry and Dave, after their reconnaissance trip, had reported that the bull terrier was inside the kennel with the four other dogs, so they knew that they hadn't missed the men's departure. Their chosen position, behind bramble bushes at the far end of the large barn, offered easy concealment combined with a clear view of the yard and the dog kennel. All it lacked was shelter, Elaine thought ruefully, pushing damp tendrils of hair away from her face. Rainwater was spiralling down Kate's corkscrew curls and dripping off the ends, and Mike had to keep taking his glasses off and drying them on the sleeve of his sweater.

Kate was remarking, "If they are going to do anything today, surely they won't leave it much later," when suddenly Stuart's voice on the radio made them all jump. He reported that a van with two men in it had just passed and was heading towards the farm. Almost as soon as Mike signed off, the sound of an engine was heard at the gate, and the dogs barked from the kennels in recognition as the short terrier man got out to unfasten the padlock. The other man drove the van in, and the short one locked the padlock again.

"That must mean they're not going anywhere," Kate whispered. "They wouldn't bother to lock up if they were going straight out again."

The tall thin man, having parked the van and locked it up – which seemed to confirm what Kate had said – now joined the shorter one in the yard, and they walked across to the kennels. They disappeared inside for some minutes before the tall man emerged and, to the consternation of the three concealed watchers, walked straight towards them. However, he turned past the veal unit, had a quick look along the footpath, and called out, "It's OK, Ted. No one about."

The short man came out of the kennel with a sturdy white bull terrier on a stout leash. He led it within yards of the watchers, so close that Elaine could see the bull terrier's tattered ears and scarred chest. The dog turned towards them and growled faintly, and Elaine's heart plummeted. Were they to be discovered at this early stage?

But Ted jerked at the dog's leash roughly, saying to his companion, "Rabbits, I s'pose. Come on, Boxer, you've got work to do."

"He'll save his energy, if he's any sense," said the thin man, in the more cultured voice Elaine remembered from the farmyard encounter. "Let's get a move on. We're late already."

They strode away, followed by the surprised eyes of the onlookers. As soon as they were out of earshot, Mike contacted Stuart to relate what had happened.

"As they've gone on foot – and if they *are* going to a dog-fight – then it means it's one of the other farms on the estate," Kate muttered to Elaine. "Christ! And we're the only ones without a map. But we must be able to narrow it down to two or three places."

"They won't be going along the footpath, surely," Elaine muttered back. "Anyone might see them. What should we do – follow them on foot, or wait for the others?"

"Stuart says, if we follow them – carefully – the others'll go round by road," Mike reported after a hasty conversation. "He agrees there's only one or two places possible. They can't be going far."

The dampness and drizzle probably provided favourable conditions, Elaine thought as they hurried up the track; the men wouldn't be inclined to hang around, and there was no wind to carry their scent to the dog. She had been right in her guess – the men turned off the footpath almost immediately, keeping to a hedgerow beside a ploughed field. She, Mike and Kate waited until the men had passed through a gap at the top of the field before jogging in pursuit. It was like the hunting again, except that this time it was more serious, their quarry more deadly. The rain pattered into her face and she felt the dampness of it seeping through the shoulders of her jacket, but she was glad to be moving after the cold wait, doing something positive. They made their way through a wood and across several fields, always keeping the men and the dog just in sight.

Their destination proved to be only about a mile away, a small farm, unsuitably picturesque, with a red-tiled farmhouse sheltering beneath a spreading blue-green cedar tree. The farm had a cluster of tiled outbuildings, and was sheltered in a lonely spot at the end of a mud track. Ideal for a dog-fight, Elaine thought; there was hardly the remotest chance of anyone coming near on a damp Sunday afternoon. The followers paused behind a hedge at the top of a field of winter wheat, and watched until they saw the two men go up to the farmhouse door, speak to someone inside, and then take their dog into the largest of the outhouses, a timbered barn, followed by three other men from the house. There were two cars parked in the farmyard.

"It *must* be a dog-fight," Elaine said. "They wouldn't be taking their bull terrier out on a mere social call in someone's barn on a wet Sunday."

"We've got enough evidence to call the police, now," Kate pointed out. "We've even seen the dog with the scars on it."

Mike grinned, wiping his glasses again. "Terry'll kill you if you do. He's been looking forward to this."

So has Mark, Elaine thought, while Mike contacted the others to describe their whereabouts.

Stuart, finding somewhere on the map which matched the description Mike gave, suggested that they all met up at the lane approaching the farm, where it ran through a wood about a third of a mile uphill.

"Look!" Kate said suddenly, grabbing Elaine's arm.

Following the direction of Kate's pointing finger, Elaine saw a man in dark clothes coming out of the barn, and taking up a standing position under the eaves of the stable block. He lit up a cigarette, apparently preparing to wait for some time.

"He must be the lookout," Kate said. "Stuart said they'd be bound to have one."

Mike nodded. "Well, it'll be easier for us if we know where he is. Let's hope there's just the one."

The rendezvous in the wood was accomplished, all three cars already parked by the roadside by the time

Elaine and Mike and Kate arrived, muddy and soaked. They reported the whereabouts of the lookout and everyone considered what to do next.

"A few of us – say four – had better go down there first," Terry suggested. "Now we know where the lookout is, we can go down the side of the field and in round the back. Then if the coast's clear, we'll wave to the rest of you."

"Remember there may be someone else in the house," Stuart warned.

Terry obviously wanted to be one of the advance party, and with him went Dave, Pete and Mark, who had his camera gear hidden inside his jacket. The others walked with them as far as a vantage point behind a tall hedge which offered concealment, should it be necessary. Now that a confrontation seemed imminent, Elaine found herself feeling strangely calm. Everything was going remarkably well so far. Only five men had been seen to enter the barn, a reasonable number to confront, although presumably there must have been at least one other dog already inside. She shivered, cold and uncomfortable in her damp clothes, thankful that the drizzle had slackened to a fine mist.

At last Pete reappeared at the back of barn, gesturing for the others to follow. They cautiously made their way down the far side of the hedgerow, and climbed through the sagging fence behind the barn, where thistles and nettles and brambles grew in profusion. Pete waited for them; the others were nowhere to be seen.

"We've taken care of the lookout," he whispered. "But we'll have to watch out in case they send someone else out."

"What do you mean, 'taken care of'?" Stuart whispered back anxiously.

Pete grinned wickedly. "Persuaded him to have a little rest, like. He's tied up in an empty stable. Well, what did you expect us to do?" he asked, seeing Elaine's shocked expression. "Hand him an RSPCA leaflet? We've left Dave round there with him, and Terry and Mark have gone round the back. There's a place round the side where we can get in among the brambles and maybe see what's going on."

Elaine wondered anxiously what they had done to the lookout. She wished Stuart had gone on with Mark, to exert his steadying influence, so that Terry and Pete hadn't had the opportunity of taking charge. She followed the others towards the side wall of the barn, treading as softly as she could, avoiding clutching brambles and cracking twigs. Robin was ahead of her, and she wondered what he thought of the afternoon's outing. It looked like being a fairly eventful introduction to Animal Rights. She didn't think he'd be much use if it did come to a fight – he was thin and frail, probably less tough than she was herself.

The barn was, fortunately, an old one, with irregular timbers affording cracks and even one or two knotholes through which they could peer into the barn. Even so, it was difficult to make out what was happening inside. Elaine could hear men's voices and distinguish figures moving about, but how many men were there, and what exactly they were doing, she couldn't have said. There didn't seem to be any dog-fighting yet; she could hear muffled conversations and the occasional coarse laugh, but nothing to suggest that a life-and-death struggle was taking place.

Robin, on Elaine's left, whispered, "I can't see a thing. It's all straw bales down this end."

Mike, who had just realized the same thing, was tiptoeing back to Elaine's end, towards the front half of the barn. "Mark and Terry are going in," he told her quietly.

"*In?*"

125

"There's a small door at the back, and the back half of the barn is full of bales of hay. They're going to creep in and climb over the top of the bales. They say they won't get any photos otherwise."

Elaine stared at him, aghast. "They're mad! It's too dangerous."

Mike shrugged. "There's no way anyone's going to stop them."

Elaine looked round anxiously for Kate and Stuart. There was no sign of them; they must have decided to go round to the other side of the barn. Robin, who by standing on tiptoe had found a better crack to look through, waved to her frantically. "I think something's about to start," he told her. "I can see a sort of ring marked out with old doors and boards, and I can see at least five dogs in there, all bull terriers, I think. You look," he suggested to Mike, who was a good six inches taller. "You'll be able to see more."

Elaine searched desperately for a crack to look through. Next moment, there could be no doubt that a fight had started; threats and shouts of encouragement were heard, and Elaine thought she could distinguish muffled growls and scuffles from the dogs themselves. She remembered reading that dog-fighting sessions often began with "rolls", or minor bouts for the younger dogs, as a preliminary to the main fight, on which money would be staked. She thought of poor Boxer, with his scarred chest and ears. He looked like a seasoned fighter, and was probably being reserved for the main event.

Mike backed away from his spyhole, looking shaken. "Christ!" he said, in appalled tones. "There's at least *fifteen* men in there!"

"Fifteen?" Robin echoed in a barely audible whisper.

Elaine stared at him in dismay. "And Mark's probably inside by now!" If they were discovered, it would be ten of them, including three girls, against fifteen hefty men – and

126

men who knew full well they'd face heavy fines or even imprisonment if they were caught. They'll pulverize us, Elaine thought desperately. She wondered whether any of the dog-fighters had weapons – knives, perhaps, or even guns. It wasn't a pleasant thought, but then the idea occurred to her that Terry and some of the others might have weapons of their own. She didn't know whether this made it better or worse, fearing an escalation of violence. What utter fools we were, thinking we could take on a gang of criminals, she thought bitterly.

A sudden flurry of activity from within drove these recriminations from her head. A prolonged squealing from one of the dogs was greeted by yells of encouragement from the spectators inside. Mike leapt back to his crack. "The bastards!" he fumed.

"What's happening?" Elaine demanded, interrupting his impotent raging.

"One of the dogs has got the other on its back and it's biting its throat . . . the bastards love it, listen . . . no one's trying to separate them . . ."

It was a torture to have to stand there waiting, listening to the terrified squealing. Elaine, a sudden desire for righteous violence surging through her, wished she could rush in and smash the men's heads against the wall. Any fines or imprisonment they might receive would be ludicrously inadequate as a punishment for deliberately making animals mutilate each other.

"It's up . . . but bleeding badly . . . they're going for each other again . . ." Mike reported.

"There's plenty of noise to cover up whatever Mark's doing, anyway," Robin pointed out.

After a few moments more, the present fight ended, confirming Elaine's guess that it was just a preliminary. Crouching and squinting, she managed to see through a slit at about knee height that a new pair of dogs were being brought into the ring. Unfortunately, her position was so low down that the wooden boards which formed the sides of the ring obscured her view of what was happening inside it, and she could only tell by the renewed excitement of the men, and the grunts and scuffles of the dogs, that a second fight was beginning. She could see the dog which had been wounded in the first fight, tied to a post, its short white coat spattered with blood from the wounds in its chest and ears. No one seemed to be doing anything about its injuries, the men all giving their attention to a new contest. A man was standing inside the ring – the referee, she supposed – and she recognized Ted, the shorter of the two men from the veal farm. What a photograph, if Mark could get it! There could be no denying the man's involvement if he were pictured actually officiating at a fight.

"What's happening?" Robin whispered.

"There's a second fight," she whispered back.

"They seem to be evenly matched," Mike reported from his superior vantage point. "They're snapping at each other's head and jaws, but neither one is really getting a hold."

"Do you think Mark's inside by now? Can you see anything?"

"Can't see from here, but I should imagine so."

What were Kate and Stuart doing, Elaine wondered. Why had they disappeared without saying anything? She hoped they hadn't been waylaid by some patrolling dog-fighter. But a glance towards the barn doors reassured her on that point. She could see that they were latched shut on the inside, so that she would have seen or heard anyone coming out.

The second bout seemed to be ending now. The men's shouts and jeers had died down, and the two dogs were brought out of the ring, both bleeding from bite wounds to the head and ears. Now, it seemed, the main fight of the day was to take place. The thin terrier man led Boxer into

128

the ring, and his opponent, a dark brindled dog, thickset and much scarred, was led in after him. This time, the handlers of both dogs stayed in the ring, as well as the referee. Elaine could hear a buzz of earnest conversation, punctuated by jeers and laughter – the men were placing bets, she supposed.

"How long do you think this one will last?" Robin asked Mike.

"Probably much longer than the others, if it's the main fight. I think they just let them carry on fighting until the ref decides on a result." Mike was looking distinctly anxious, chewing a thumbnail. "I hope Terry and Mark have the sense to get some photos quickly and come out. We don't want to be here when they pack up for the day."

Elaine thought of the three cars parked just a short distance along the lane. If any of the men did leave, they would be sure to realize what was going on, and would probably come back. There was no alternative but to wait. They couldn't leave now, with Mark inside.

The fight was beginning, the handlers stepping back, urging their dogs to the attack with harsh commands. Elaine could hear the grunts of the dogs, and the scraping sounds of their claws on the concrete floor. She found herself irrationally sticking up for Boxer, hoping he wouldn't come off worse. The brindled dog looked so menacing, a scarred veteran of countless fights. Even so, she knew it was stupid to dislike it for its looks and its temperament; they were by-products of selective breeding, genetically engineered for human ends, just like the tiny toy dogs at the other end of the spectrum. She knew that it was unlikely to be a fight to the death – good fighting dogs were too valuable for their owners to let them be killed, when they could patch them up and make them fight again, to win more betting money.

There was a long scuffle, both dogs snarling, to the accompaniment of excited cheers from the watchers inside, and then a long agonized squeal rose above the general noise, setting Elaine's teeth on edge. At the same moment, Mike beside her gave an exclamation of surprise. "Christ, there's Mark – I can see his head and shoulders, right at the front of the hay bales – the men'll see him –"

Elaine found her knee-high crack just in time to see one of the tied dogs lunge frantically towards the back of the barn, with deep, threatening barks. One of the watchers at the ringside turned, saw Mark hastily retreating and gave a shout of alarm, and the next moment all the men were hurling themselves towards the hay bales, the fight forgotten.

"God – they'll kill him –" Mike, his face aghast, turned blindly towards the front of the barn.

"No – the doors are locked from the inside!" Elaine shouted. In a blind panic she ran with the others to the low back door of the barn. Hardly knowing what they were planning to do, she squeezed through the door, grappling for handfuls of hay and heaving herself to the top of the stack. Stuart had appeared from somewhere, she was relieved to see, and with him and Mike ahead of her she half-crawled, half-ran across the hay, cursing as her leg slipped down between bales, picking herself up and struggling on again. At the front of the stack, bales had been removed forming a gradual descent; Terry was lying half-on, half-off the stack, and as Elaine crawled closer she could see that a hefty, red-faced man had him by the neck of his jacket, almost choking him, and was trying to pull him down. Stuart grabbed hold of Terry's legs and held on firmly. The man, seeing Stuart, and the others behind him, stared open-mouthed and shouted to his friends, "There are dozens of the buggers!"

Elaine, desperately scanning the inside of the barn for Mark, was just in time to see one of the two men who were holding him jerk his camera roughly from around his

130

neck and smash it viciously against the barn wall. Another man ran up to join in, and two of them held Mark while the third, flinging the smashed camera contemptuously aside, walked coolly up and swung his fist violently into Mark's face. Elaine watched, horrified and helpless, as Mark's head jerked back sickeningly and the men let him crash to the floor, where all three of them kicked him in the ribs with evident enjoyment.

"Oh, Mark, Mark . . ." Elaine's voice came in broken sobs. Pete, Mike and Dave threw themselves on the three men, trying to drag them away from Mark; the man who was struggling with Terry, momentarily distracted, loosened his grip. Terry, clutching his throat, slithered off the stack and threw himself into the fray, followed by Stuart.

Elaine had been momentarily paralysed with shock at the violence. Now, regaining the use of her legs, she jumped down the bales to floor level and ran to where Mark lay groaning and only semiconscious, blood streaming from his nose and split lip. There was no time to do anything for him. She looked up; men were untying ropes . . .

"The dogs!" she yelled in alarm.

The bull terriers, who had been straining impotently at their leashes, were now loose and advancing menacingly, eyes glinting and ragged lips snarling. They ought to be on our side, Elaine found herself thinking stupidly. The next moment it seemed to her that she was thrown into the middle of a welter of flying fists, grabbing hands and snapping jaws. It was difficult to distinguish individuals in the mass of brawling figures. She saw Pete roll to the floor in front of her, felled by a vicious blow, and two of the men had hold of Mike, one of them snatching off his glasses and crushing them underfoot.

Trying to stay upright but knocked off balance by a cannoning body, she gave a yell of fright as sharp teeth sank into her leg. It was the huge brindled dog, she registered in panic; mercifully, it unlocked its jaws and she pulled free before it seized another mouthful, this time only fastening on to her jeans. As she tried to pull away, the dog held firm, snarling, its front legs braced. The damp fabric ripped, and she broke free, but the dog held her at bay, snarling if she moved any further away.

Pinioned, she looked up, shielding her face from accidental blows, and took stock of the situation.

The intruders were herded together by the hay bales, several of them winded or bitten. Grins of anticipation were beginning to spread as the dog-fighters realized that their opponents were too few in number to offer further resistance. Mark still lay lifeless on the ground, and Pete was struggling to a sitting position, groaning and clutching his stomach; Mike was clasping an injured shoulder. Sandra, who had found a short thick pole from somewhere, was waving it about threateningly at anyone who approached. Where the hell was Kate? Elaine hadn't seen her since they'd entered the barn.

She looked at their captors' evil grins with foreboding. For a panic-stricken moment she thought the men were going to kill them. They were, after all, in a desperate position, for all their temporary advantage in terms of numbers. They knew that their venue had been discovered and that the intruders had had a good look at several of their faces, good enough to identify them again. While these thoughts were flashing through Elaine's mind, she realized that the men themselves were equally uncertain as to what to do. They seemed to be looking for guidance towards the beefy, red-faced man who'd been grappling with Terry. He was now grinning maliciously and looking at Terry, who was standing a little apart from the others, winded from a punch in the stomach. "That's the one I want," the man said with relish.

"Bait 'im, Henry," called out one of the others, causing a few appreciative laughs.

"Shut it, you fool," the big man snapped, presumably angry at being addressed by name. "Leave this to me."

There was an ominous silence as he approached Terry with slow menacing steps. What was he going to do, Elaine wondered frantically. Beat up Terry as they had done Mark, while the others watched, restrained and helpless? But Henry's intentions were never made clear. Terry's hand flew to his pocket and next moment he was brandishing a knife.

"Terry, no!" cried Sandra behind him.

Henry, smiling sardonically, stepped back. "That's your game, is it?"

Everyone seemed frozen to the spot. Terry, the initiative now on his side, advanced slowly, his eyes, steely cold, fixed on Henry. Several of the other men moved forward threateningly. It could only end in disaster, Elaine thought.

"For God's sake put that away, you fool," Stuart shouted harshly.

"Set the dogs on 'im," said the man who had spoken before. "'E won't use 'is knife on them. 'E's an animal lover."

Henry gave a curt nod of agreement. Terry's eyes flashed defensively from side to side as the handlers quietly called their dogs to them. He looked indecisive, in a cleft stick, Elaine thought; he either had to stand there and be mauled, or use his knife on the dogs. The bull terriers stood beside their handlers, snarling ominously, waiting for the command to attack.

Suddenly Stuart's voice rang out, calm and authoritative. "I don't think I'd do that, if I were in your position. The police will be arriving at any moment."

Henry swivelled round to face Stuart. An expression of doubt flickered across his face, quickly replaced by one of arrogant amusement. "You're bluffing," he sneered.

Stuart gazed back steadily. "Tell yourself that, if you like," he said diffidently. "We've nothing to lose."

There was a pregnant silence in the barn, broken only by

the faint snarls of the dogs. Stuart *must* be bluffing, Elaine knew, but he was certainly convincing enough, staring at Henry with contempt. It was Henry who was beginning to look slightly less in command, his supercilious smile wavering.

One of the men behind him jerked his dog back nervously. "Shit, Henry, if the little bleeder's really gone and called the police . . ." he began. Elaine could hear the unmistakable note of fear in his voice; Stuart's inspired lie had deceived him, at least. "Let's get the dogs out while there's time."

"He's bluffing," Henry repeated, sounding much less certain.

Terry was still braced ready for action, grasping his knife firmly, some of the dogs still eyeing him. Mike and Dave and the others were trying not to betray their surprise, Elaine thought, everyone watching the men's reactions. Obviously Stuart had aimed to throw the men into confusion, diverting their attention from dealing with the intruders. Indeed, several of the men were now pulling their dogs back, fastening their leashes. "Sid's right," said Ted. "I'm not waiting about if the fuzz are on the way. Get all the dogs out."

Henry looked anxiously from face to face, seeing his support dwindling. "Hang about," he snapped angrily. "What are we going to do about our friends here?"

Stuart, actually smiling, Elaine noticed with incredulity, said quietly, "I don't think you need worry," and in the silence which followed this baffling remark, all eyes swivelled to face the main doors at the sound of car engines in the farmyard.

"In here," shouted Kate's voice outside.

Footsteps tramped across the yard and the barn door was shaken vigorously.

"Open up this door," an authoritative voice commanded. "This is the police."

Chapter Eleven

Elaine sat on the bus, staring sightlessly out of the window. She would normally have been travelling in the opposite direction at this time of the afternoon, on the bus home from school, but she hadn't been to school today. It had been very late last night by the time she had had her bitten leg attended to and finished answering questions at the police station, and she had felt too drained, emotionally and physically, to face a day at school and a rehearsal of *As You Like It*.

Her parents didn't know she had stayed at home, and that was one more thing she was going to have to explain later that evening. It wasn't a pleasant thought. She had only spoken to them briefly the night before, in a hasty telephone call from the police station, and in a terse exchange when she'd finally arrived home, past midnight. She'd been thankful then when they'd said that full explanations could wait until the following day, but now that the evening was drawing closer she felt distinctly apprehensive. "Foolish bravado" was the most generous interpretation they were likely to put on the dog-fighting escapade.

In fact, that was how the police had seen it, and in the light of what had happened Elaine herself felt that she and her friends had been unbelievably naïve to behave as they had. In retrospect, she could see that it would have been so simple, having tracked the men as far as the barn, to have called the police at that stage; or, when Terry had first mentioned the dog-fighting, they could have contacted the RSPCA or the League Against Cruel Sports, who were experienced at dealing with such things. Instead, they had stupidly endangered themselves by thinking they could outwit a bunch of hardened criminals. Elaine shrank from thinking what might have happened if the police hadn't arrived when they did. The situation had been desperate, with Terry about to defend himself with his knife against the attacking dogs (she was in little doubt that he would have done so, if the only alternative was to be, at the least, badly mauled – and she knew only too well how painful a single bite from those iron jaws could be). And what might the men not have done then, if he had defended himself, seeing their valuable fighting dogs mauled or killed? It had been a horrible situation, an Animal Rights campaigner forced to defend himself against the very creatures he was trying to save. Elaine asked herself what she would have done; it was easy enough to say that you would respond with Gandhian passivity, but what would you do if really faced with the situation?

It was only thanks to Kate, who had driven Stuart's car to the nearest village phone-box (unmindful of her pro-visional driving licence and the fact that she had had only two driving lessons), that the dogs were now safely in custody, and the men facing trial and prosecution, but that could have been done without any of them entering the barn and risking their own safety. The whole affair had been totally bungled, and the main culprit, she had to admit, was Mark, who had insisted that they confront the dog-fighters themselves. Ironically, Mark himself was the worst casualty, and had been kept in hospital with con-cussion and cracked ribs and severe bruising; he would probably be allowed out the next day. Apart from that, the tally of injuries consisted of dog bites (received by several people), a black eye and cut lip (Pete), and a broken collar bone (Mike).

The bus was nearly empty before Elaine realized that it had reached the town centre, the end of its route. She got off and made her way towards the hospital, pausing to buy

136

a bunch of black grapes and a paperback book for Mark. Her critical mood evaporated to be replaced by one of sympathy as she thought of him lying in a hospital bed, probably as upset by his broken camera as by his broken ribs. And if he too had been struck by the foolhardiness of the venture into which he had led the others, that would only add to the total of his discomfort.

Her step quickened as she entered the hospital gates, glad at the prospect of having him to herself for an hour. She had hardly had a chance to speak to him the day before, and her last glimpse had been of his bruised and bloody face as he was carried into an ambulance, wrapped in a scarlet blanket.

Hurrying past signs pointing out the x-ray, ultrasound and maternity departments, she found her way to Mark's ward. She hesitated at the entrance, assailed by the sudden warmth, her nostrils assimilating an aroma compounded of floor cleaner and boiled cabbage. A clock above the ward entrance showed that she was a few minutes late; other visitors were already inside, sitting round beds. She couldn't see Mark. A scurrying nurse saw her hesitation and looked at her enquiringly.

"I've come to visit Mark Harrington."

"Mark Harrington? He's in the last bed on the right."

Elaine walked past the neat rows of beds with their trolleys laden with get-well cards and flowering pot plants. Catching sight of Mark sitting up in the end bed, she almost stopped in her tracks – he already had a visitor. Sitting close to the bed-head, with her back towards the ward, was someone who looked very much like Caroline Radway.

Elaine bit her lip with annoyance. How had Caroline known Mark was here, and why had she come? Now she would have to sit and make polite conversation instead of having a private talk with Mark. She had almost forgotten Caroline, having forgiven Mark's flirtation, but if Caroline intended to make such an obvious play for him she knew he would find it hard to resist.

Mark looked up somewhat furtively as she approached. He looked awful, his lower lip swollen and purplish, and a large tri-coloured bruise spreading lopsidedly across his cheek from his nose to his swollen left eyelid. Caroline, facing the bed, didn't notice Elaine, but following Mark's gaze she turned and gave her the pleasantest of smiles. She looked enviably pretty, her short blonde hair sleekly styled, her large hazel eyes enhanced with make-up. Elaine detected a waft of expensive perfume – for Mark's benefit, she thought cattily.

"Hallo, Elaine," Mark said rather awkwardly. "You two have seen each other, haven't you, at rehearsals?"

"Yes," Elaine said. "And at the opening meet," she added pointedly, in case Mark had forgotten that Caroline was on the enemy's side. She crossed to the far side of the bed, bent down to kiss Mark's uninjured cheek, to his obvious discomfiture, and gave him her two packages.

"Pull up a chair," he suggested.

Caroline watched Elaine, intrigued, as she did so. "You're one of Mark's friends from the Animal Rights group, aren't you?"

"Yes, that's right." Elaine hoped that Mark would say something to indicate that she was more than that, but he remained silent, looking at the book she had given him.

"I think it was so brave of you all, to tackle the dog-fighters," Caroline continued. "I was horrified when I realized that dog-fighting was actually taking place on one of our local farms. I mean, you read about it in the papers, but you never think of it actually going on, do you? I think it's terrible, absolutely barbaric."

Elaine stared at her in disbelief. How could someone who actually took part in a blood sport expect to make such remarks with any degree of credibility?

"It seems two of the hunt terrier men were involved," she couldn't resist saying.

138

Caroline's gaze was somewhat less friendly as she faced Elaine across the bed. "Well, *if* that were true, the hunt would dismiss them at once. The British Field Sports Society is absolutely against illegal sports."

"Obviously not all its members feel the same." Elaine turned to Mark for support, but he refused to be drawn in, saying instead, "At least these particular men are bound to be convicted and fined, if not imprisoned."

"What do you think they'll get?" Caroline asked.

"Judging by previous cases, fines of about £500 with perhaps a couple of months' imprisonment," Mark replied.

"Is that all?" Elaine was horrified. "But that's pathetic! A couple of months? And £500 – they must make more than that, betting and selling dogs!"

"It doesn't seem very much," Caroline agreed.

Mark shrugged, then winced with pain from his cracked ribs. "No. I doubt if it would stop them from carrying on when they come out of prison. They'll most likely be barred from keeping dogs for about five years, but that won't stop them. If they're caught with a dog, they've only got to say it belongs to their wife or their brother. Now that there are no dog licences, who can prove anything?"

Elaine was stunned into silence. All along she had imagined that, if the men were caught, they would receive punishments imposing enough to put an end to the dog-fighting for good. Now, it seemed that at best they had brought about a temporary halt to the men's bloodthirsty pastime.

"Will it be in the papers?" Caroline asked.

"It might get a mention in the nationals, particularly when the trial comes up. And it'll certainly be in the *Gazette* this week. A couple of reporters came in and interviewed me this morning, and took my photograph." Mark gave a painful lopsided grin. "Pity I'm not looking my debonair best, really, isn't it?" He looked into a small mirror which stood on his bedside cabinet, ruefully fingering his swollen lip.

"I think it was so brave of you," Caroline said again. She turned to Elaine. "When Mark told me on Saturday night what he was planning to do, I tried to talk him out of it – I thought it was too dangerous – but he still insisted."

Elaine thought her ears must be deceiving her. Mark opened his mouth to say something, but she cut in, "On Saturday night?"

"Yes, Mark and I went out for a meal," Caroline confirmed, "and he told me all about it then."

Elaine turned to Mark with an accusing stare. He flushed slightly, his eyes sliding away, unable to meet her gaze. She bit back the words, "I thought you were going out with some friends from college?", her pride just stopping her in time from revealing to Caroline that Mark had lied to her.

"I didn't know you were at art college," she said to Caroline, instead.

Caroline gave her a strange look. "Who said anything about art college? Of course I'm not, I'm still at school, as you know."

"Sorry, I must have made a mistake," Elaine said with a venomous glance at Mark.

"Of course, the first thing I did this morning was phone the flat to see what had happened, and Mark's flatmate told me he was in here," Caroline continued, apparently unaware of Elaine's fury and Mark's discomfiture. "Your Mr Parsonage was furious at the rehearsal today – a second bedridden Orlando. Of course, everyone told him Mark would be fully recovered in time to save the day."

Elaine hardly registered what Caroline was saying. She felt speechless with indignation, her brain seething with the thoughts chasing each other round her head. It wasn't just the personal disloyalty Mark had shown, lying to her while planning to go out with someone else. Just as bad

140

was the fact that he had risked the whole show by telling Caroline, who was a known hunt supporter and might very well be on friendly terms with the terrier men, for all Mark knew. Why had he told her anything about it at all? Purely to win her admiration, to portray himself as a hero, Elaine answered herself bitterly.

Caroline was chatting brightly about the rehearsal, though neither Elaine nor Mark were paying much attention. She was wearing a very expensive-looking, beautifully-cut suede jacket, of a soft mushroom beige. Looking at it, Elaine remembered that Mark had a suede jacket, although none of the other Animal Rights members would be seen dead in one. She listened to Caroline until she could stand it no longer. She stood up abruptly.

"You're not going already, are you?" Mark looked dismayed.

"Yes. I've got a lot to do tonight."

"You can't come back later, I suppose? There's a visiting hour from seven to eight." He turned his most imploring gaze on her.

She looked away quickly. "No, sorry. I'm too busy. There's an Animal Rights meeting tomorrow, but I don't suppose you'll be going, will you? You seem to have switched sides."

She walked defiantly out of the ward and found her way towards the hospital exit, the cold air of the late afternoon striking her face in contrast to the dry, overheated atmosphere inside. In the shrubberies, sombre with laurel and holly, a blackbird called out its mournful warning note. Elaine walked on quickly at first, carried by the impetus of her dramatic exit. But her pace slowed as her righteous indignation faded, to be replaced by a sense of utter loss.

She realized now that she had always expected this to happen. She had known that Mark's interest in her wouldn't last, that his affections were no more durable than the hothouse blooms in the hospital ward. Yet this knowledge hadn't been enough to lessen the emotional investment she had made in him.

The thought that his fascination for Caroline was likely to be equally short-lived did little to console her. She dragged her feet, scuffing up dead leaves from the path, and fought back her tears. How could she recover from such a blow, pick herself up and carry on as before, going to school, doing her homework and rehearsing the play, when it seemed to her that there was a gaping empty hole in the centre of her life?

In the town centre, the Christmas lights were already up, casting a festive glow on the crowds hurrying from offices and stores. Elaine walked past the tinsel dazzle of the window displays, her mood more suitable for a funeral than for Christmas preparations. She was too occupied with her thoughts even to glower at a women who brushed past her wearing an opulent fur coat. Mark's lack of commitment to Animal Rights upset her just as much as his betrayal of her trust. At the veal farm, she remembered, he had been driven by a sense of adventure, not, as she had been, by outrage at the calves' conditions; it had been the same last night. To him, she thought savagely, there was no difference between raiding a dog-fight and playing Orlando in the play. They were both ways of being the centre of attention.

Realizing that someone was walking towards her, she jerked her thoughts abruptly back to the present. It was Alistair, tall and lanky in a dark raincoat, carrying his flute in its case.

"Elaine! Are you all right?" He was looking at her in concern.

She managed a weak smile. "Yes, I'm fine, thanks. I'm just going to catch the bus. Are you going home now?"

"No. I'm on my way to wind band." He looked at her doubtfully. "Are you sure you're all right? You looked as if you were walking along in a daze."

142

"I suppose I was, really." She blinked rapidly in an attempt to conceal the traces of her tears, resisting the temptation to throw herself into Alistair's arms and sob hysterically. "I was just annoyed about something, that's all."

"Is it –" Alistair hesitated. "Is it about Mark and that Caroline girl?"

Elaine stared at him, taken aback. "How do you know? I've only just found out myself."

"She was talking about it at the rehearsal – about Mark and the dog-fight, I mean. The way she was talking made it sound as though Mark had done the whole thing single-handed, as well as giving the impression that she and Mark were thick as thieves. She didn't know Kate had been in on it, too. Old Kate was pretty shocked, you can imagine. She had a real go at Caroline – told her you can't run with the hare and hunt with the hounds."

"Very appropriate," Elaine commented dryly, thinking with affection of Kate, who was as remorseless as a bull terrier herself in defence of her friends and her principles. "Kate was the real heroine, whatever Caroline said about Mark. She was the one who had the sense to go and get the police."

"Is your leg all right? She said you'd been bitten."

"It hurts a bit, but it's OK, thanks. I was lucky only to be bitten once."

"Sounds like it." Alistair glanced at his watch. "Look, I must go. You haven't forgotten about the concert, have you, on the 18th? I said I'd get you a ticket. Sita's coming as well, but you like her, don't you?"

"Of course I do. Thanks – I'd love to come. Thank you for remembering."

She walked on, warmed by Alistair's kindness. A less sympathetic person, having been rejected in favour of Mark, would have said "Serves you right." She thought guiltily of the unfair comparisons she'd made between the

143

two, seeing Alistair as dull and conventional. But she realized now that he had other qualities she hadn't valued at the time. She knew that Alistair would never be any more to her than a friend, but she knew now that friendship wasn't to be undervalued.

She would phone Kate when she got in, she decided, and talk about the aftermath of the dog-fight (though she wouldn't talk about her shattered feelings for Mark, even to Kate), and about the forthcoming Animal Rights meeting. With Christmas approaching, there would be 'ew campaigns against fur coats and turkey farming. There was always something to fight against.

She was accustomed by now to the familiar wave of depression at the sheer variety and scale of the suffering man caused to animals – vivisection, factory farming, hunting, the fur industry – and the apparent indifference of most of the animal-loving public. But this time, a new, stubborn determination won through.

"I *will* carry on fighting," she told herself fiercely.

It was more than a passing phase with her, she felt strongly. It was a consuming passion, stronger even than her wounded feelings over Mark. She would continue to campaign, no matter how great the difficulties may be. Perhaps she would even make it her career, if she could be lucky enough to find a job with one of the animal welfare organizations. She could do it properly then – find out all the facts, and be in a position to work for long-term improvements, instead of squandering her efforts in amateurish flounderings.

It would give her purpose enough to last several lifetimes, she reckoned.

She walked on quickly towards the bus stop, past the butcher's shop with its dangling naked turkeys and its slabs of cold animal flesh.